Fall in !

Holding On For A Hero

VIKINGS ROCK!

Book 2

by Lily Harlem

"Sex, Drugs, & Rock 'n' Row

DRAGONBLADE PUBLISHING, INC.

ARE YOU SIGNED UP FOR DRAGONBLADE'S BLOG?

You'll get the latest news and information on exclusive giveaways, exclusive excerpts, coming releases, sales, free books, cover reveals and more.

Check out our complete list of authors, too!

No spam, no junk. That's a promise!

Sign Up Here

www.dragonbladepublishing.com

Dearest Reader;

Thank you for your support of a small press. At Dragonblade Publishing, we strive to bring you the highest quality Historical Romance from some of the best authors in the business. Without your support, there is no 'us', so we sincerely hope you adore these stories and find some new favorite authors along the way.

Happy Reading!

CEO, Dragonblade Publishing

Additional Dragonblade books by
Author Lily Harlem

VIKINGS ROCK!
Bats Out of Hell (Book 1)
Holding On for a Hero (Book 2)

Hawk Castle Series
Loved by the Last Knight (Book 1)
Adored by the Archduke (Book 2)
Embraced by the Emperor (Book 3)

The Lyon's Den Series
Lyon at the Altar

Recap of Book One:
Bats Out of Hell

Did you read *BATS OUT OF HELL*, the story of Haakon and Kenna? Of course you did. That's why you're here. But it might have been a while ago, so here's a quick recap of Book One in the VIKINGS ROCK! series.

In the far north, the land of Vikings, the Rhalson family is splintered apart when Ravn takes the crown from his twin brother, Haakon. Unable to live under his brother's rule, Haakon, along with his brother Orm; sister, Astrid; and a few loyal and strong friends, sails away in the pursuit of a new kingdom to rule.

When they land, or rather wash up, on the shores of Lothlend, the first thing Haakon sees is a beautiful Valkyrie about to take him to the heavenly realm of Valhalla. Except Kenna is no Valkyrie; she's the spirited daughter of the local village leader.

Soon Kenna finds herself in a situation where she must marry Haakon, the new and self-proclaimed King of Tillicoulty, in order to prevent him and his pagan friends from slaying her fellow villagers. She has one demand of her own: he must become Christian.

During their turbulent relationship, the threat of King Athol and his army arriving to retake the crown Haakon has stolen is never far away. Neither is the derision of Haakon's feisty sister, Astrid. She is furious that Haakon has forsaken the Norse gods and despairs at the devotion he shows his foreign wife and his new kingdom.

This is Astrid's story, one of frustration, resilience, passion... and ultimately, a destiny of love.

Chapter One

ASTRID'S BLOOD AND bile were boiling hot and thick in her veins and guts. She couldn't stay in Tillicoulty another minute. The small, forted village had sucked the sense from her brother Haakon, and it had blinded Orm and her fellow crew to his delusional state and addled their own simple brains.

"What the fuck?" she muttered, storming over the wet ground to a small roundhouse near the watchtower. "If Odin and Thor are watching this, they'll be plotting revenge upon us all." She huffed and gripped her bow so tightly, her fingers hurt. She'd like to grip Olaf, Tillicoulty's stupid, old priest, around his neck. How dare he talk of Valhalla? His destiny was in a foul realm far from greatness. He was a fool with his one god and his precious book. A weak and pathetic fool and she hated him.

She hated them all.

Despite the icy air, her cheeks were hot as she pushed into her temporary home and grabbed a sack. After lighting a candle, she began throwing supplies into it. It might have been winter in Lothlend, but it was nothing compared to the arctic winters in the far north she was used to surviving. She didn't need the village, or its shelter. She'd be just fine on her own. In fact, she'd be better off away from them all. Odin's ravens would report her loyalty to him, the great All Father. The path of her destiny would be untarnished and unchanged.

Gunner's and Orm's laughing faces hovered in her mind as she piled furs and blankets into the sack. They'd known their mirth would strike a flint to her temper but still, they hadn't stopped themselves.

"Bloody idiots," she muttered, grabbing several candles, an earthenware bowl, and food supplies. "You'll all want my help when the wolves chase you from the gates of Valhalla, when you're not permitted entry into Asgard to feast and drink with the gods. Then you'll come running, bemoaning that you are sorry, sad, ruined, and what can I do to help."

She snatched up her runestones and attached them beside her dagger on her belt. None of her fellow Vikings had asked for a reading of late. There had been no offerings or sacrifices made, other than hers to Freya: heather, rosemary, and a small rabbit. It was as if the old ways, the true ways, had been forgotten by her fellow crew as quickly as a shooting star.

It also made her sick how quickly they'd all gotten their feet under the table with the Christian god. And how Haakon, her strong, fierce, warrior brother, went soft-eyed and agreeable whenever he was around his bride, Kenna.

What hold did Kenna have on him? Was she magic? Was she a goddess in disguise and walking the Earth as a mortal? Was Astrid failing to see something that was right in front of her?

No. Haakon was just a lovesick puppy, that was all. And it was embarrassing. She was glad her father and brother Ravn couldn't see his pathetic display of adoration; they'd have been ashamed at the way he worshipped the ground the meek Lothlender walked upon.

Astrid looked around the meager dwelling for anything else that would be of use. Soap, that would do, and a sealed urn of ale. Perhaps it would take the taste of wicked betrayal from her mouth and make her forget, for a little while at least.

She pulled her cloak hood up tightly and flung the sack over one shoulder and her bow and quiver of arrows over the other. Her shield she carried in her free hand. Then she strode out into the blustery night and stomped beneath the watchtower.

"Where are you going?" the watchman called down. "Hey, you. Stop!"

"Fuck off!" She held up one finger and kept on walking.

"There are hungry wolves out there! You won't be safe. Come back! I order you."

She ignored him and avoided the deepest puddles as she walked past the rows of winter crops the small villagers fussed over constantly. The pigpen was empty, the animals having been brought into the fort overnight.

Soon she was approaching the forest track that led to the place the villagers called "Clam Bay." It was a windy night, but the moon shone down, lighting her way. She was lucky it was full, because Máni, the moon god, had to travel swiftly to outrun the moon hound, Hati Hróðvitnisson, and soon the moon would begin to wane and the nights would be darker.

She tramped along the track, alert to the sounds around her. The screeching call of an owl cried out in the distance and the leaves blew and fluttered in a constant twist around the tree trunks.

As she went farther, the roar of the mountain river came from the east. But she turned north, back toward the shoreline, stopping only to pluck a pocketful of hazelnuts from a low-hanging tree.

Ducking her head from the icy blast, she rounded the top of a hill that signaled the end of the track. Her legs still felt pumped full of energy and with each beat, her heart squeezed with anger. But now was not the time to wander farther than necessary. The village watchman had been right: there were wolves around. She didn't need to see them or hear them to know they were there, lurking in the shadows. Sometimes she believed she could smell wolves when they were near, as though she were a creature herself.

So she'd come to the place that had been a refuge once before: the cave on the beach where she and her brothers and crew had washed up several weeks previously. It was dry and would provide shelter.

There was a stash of wood in it, and she'd spot any passing ships that might be able to take her back to Drangar.

Home.

Ja, that was what she'd do. Go home. She'd have to suck it up with Ravn as king, detestable individual that he was, but she'd at least be with her father.

Her heart softened at the thought of his smiling face and warm embrace. He was the only person who truly understood her and didn't want to change her. Why had she left him?

She peered through the ivy tendrils and into the dark cave, checking to make sure she'd be the only inhabitant. Everything was still and quiet. No peering, amber eyes or warning growl.

Quickly, she stooped and set about starting a fire in the entrance. Once the bright flames were licking upward, she spread out her furs and blanket, creating a makeshift bed on the smooth, flat rock at the back of the cave.

The ground was a mixture of tiny pebbles and sand and several dips in the rocks made for handy storage places and a shelf for candles.

But most important was security and she set her shield, bow, and arrows just to the left of the fire, where she could grab them if necessary. Her long, sharp dagger she'd keep on her person at all times.

Tomorrow, she'd set traps, collect shellfish, and gather more wood. The gods had put her on the path of a waiting game—waiting until the spring came so she could journey west and find sea passage north. Failing that, she'd go back to Tillicoulty and take one of their small fishing boats and sail herself home. *Ja*, that was what she'd do. She didn't need Haakon or Orm or any of their dumb friends. She was better off without them and could get herself anywhere she wanted to go, on her own, solo. She was an independent woman, a shield-maiden, and she had royal blood in her veins to boot.

The gods had better warn anyone who tried to stop her.

HAMISH STRUGGLED TO concentrate on the rest of the conversation that went on in the Great House. His new brother-by-law, Haakon, had continued to discuss strategy and tactics should King Athol attack the village, but Hamish found his mind wandering.

Astrid had been furious when she'd stormed out into the wild night—her cheeks almost as red as her hair and her small frame stiff with indignation. The wood scrapings she'd spilled from her lap—she'd been carving arrowheads—were still scattered on the floor like dead little beetles.

"Drink, my new brother." With a flourish that caused several splashes to land on the table, Orm filled Hamish's mug with heather ale. He was Hamish's other new brother-by-law and he was a tall, thin, wild-looking man with flashing, alert eyes ringed with kohl. "And tell us when Tillicoulty last had to fight to defend itself."

"I... We... Not in my lifetime." Hamish nodded at his father, Noah, who was looking older and greyer by the day. "We have always been compliant with King Athol and before him King Harold, and we trade peacefully with neighbors. There has been no need for bloodshed."

Gunner chuckled and tugged his thick beard. "And this is why we must hope... only small army...come here." He was picking up their language quickly, but it was still a little stilted. "Not many soldiers to kill."

"But now you have a new king." Haakon banged his broad chest and looked around the room. "One who can lead us to victory to gain full control of our lands and stop paying unjust taxes."

"I hope so." Hamish drank. He wasn't frightened of battle, or indeed death. What scared him was his family and friends getting hurt. His sister, Kenna, was insisting on fighting at Haakon's side and unbelievably, her husband didn't have a problem with that. Maybe he wasn't as doting as he led everyone to believe? Because she would surely get hurt. She was small, her muscles nothing compared to a big man's.

His attention went to Gunner's bulging muscles. He didn't wear a tunic, as was often his way around the fire, and his strength was easy to see. He'd be good to have on one's side, but if their enemy had many men of similar stature, they'd have a problem.

And Hamish's mother and father were elderly, his mother a woman. They couldn't fight, but if merciless soldiers broke into the fort, their fates would be sealed, and it wouldn't be a nice end for them.

Hamish suppressed a shudder and took another drink of ale. King Athol *would* come. It was just a matter of when.

He glanced at the door again, wondering if Astrid would return to sit and glare at everyone the way she usually did. Her ice-blue eyes were like chips from a passing glacier and her tongue as sharp as the fangs of an adder. It amazed him that all that heated passion, venom, and spirit could be packaged into such a slender petite body.

His head spun with the speed at which she could knock him or in fact anyone down with her wit and derision. Her contempt for God seemed to glow from her angry, red cheeks and her mockery of everything Christian was surely the worst blasphemy.

She spoke repeatedly of Odin, Thor, and Freya. Gods Hamish had never heard of before the Vikings had forced their way in, but these gods appeared to see everything and control each person's destiny. He'd seen her in the forest a few weeks ago, spreading heather and rosemary and a small, dead rabbit on a stone. She'd held her pretty face to the sky with hands above her head, fingers spread, as though conversing with a deity only she could see. Of course Hamish had hidden behind a tree trunk, his breath held. He knew full well she'd rip him into shreds should she find him loitering. Not that he'd meant to be spying on her; he'd been checking his traps and collecting acorns.

"Hamish."

He lifted his head and turned to Kenna. "Er, what?"

"I've been speaking to you." She frowned at him.

"Sorry, I was..." Thinking of the way the sun had caught in Astrid's hair like the last moments of a blazing, summer sunset.

"What?" she asked.

"I was wondering if you think Astrid is well?" He directed the question at Haakon. "She appeared...upset."

"Oh, don't worry about her." Orm slapped him on the back. "She's got a permanently stubbed toe."

Hamish frowned deeper. "What does that mean?"

"Her face." Orm grinned and circled his own long face. "Always sour, always twisted as if in pain."

Hamish thought her face was beautiful. Her features like a little pixie's: small, straight nose; high cheekbones; pointed chin and lips that were pouted more often than smiling, almost as if waiting to be kissed.

"It is true." Haakon laughed and took Kenna's hand in his, squeezing it. "She is not happy here. She misses our father."

Orm made a scoffing sound. "Really?"

"*Ja*, really." Haakon seemed more interested in kissing Kenna's knuckles and the underside of her wrist than continuing the conversation. "She was fond of him and he her."

"Well, at least the old fool liked someone." Orm helped himself to more bread. "Anyway, why are you worried about her, Hamish? Want to fuck her?"

"What? No." Hamish straightened. "And you shouldn't say that about your sister—it is disrespectful."

Orm nudged his shoulder onto Hamish's. "If your sister"—he pointed at Kenna—"were as belligerent, quarrelsome, and stubborn as mine, you would understand why I say what I say."

"She is a fine shield-maiden," Gunner said, drawing his thick eyebrows together.

Knud and Egil nodded at his side.

"And a capable seafarer," Ivar added. "She rows as strong and for as long as any man."

Hamish found that hard to believe, but if he was going to believe it of any woman, it would be Astrid. She was like no one he'd ever met and his fascination was growing by the day.

What made her tick? Why had she come here when she seemed to hate it so... Seemed to hate his people... Hate *him*?

And yes, she did act as though she hated him. Had done from the moment she'd seen him outside the fort on that first day.

But why? Why poke fun at him, send him withering looks, turn her back on him when he spoke? He'd done nothing wrong that he could think of.

Ivar reached across the table and took the hunk of lamb pie from Astrid's plate. He shoved it into his mouth, crumbs scattering onto his bare, inked chest and lap.

Hamish drained his ale and stood.

"Where are you going?" Kenna asked, tipping her head and studying him.

"To check on Mother. The night is cold; she might need more logs."

"I left her plenty," Noah, his father, said.

"Still, I'll check on her." Hamish pulled in a breath and walked past the Vikings and the members of council sitting taking bread and ale. He knew his mother had a good stack of firewood. She'd be sewing with her beloved dog Lass at her feet and likely sharing gossip with one of her friends. She was perfectly fine.

But he did want to check on Astrid. Make sure she was safely within the village walls. He'd get burned by her tongue for it, he was sure, but something in the way she'd stomped from the Great House so stiffly, her eyes flashing madly, had disturbed him and he couldn't shift the unease it had created.

Pulling up his tasseled hood against the wind, Hamish stomped over the wet earth, his way lit by a full moon. He passed the pigpen and the chicken coop. As he went by the stone well, a cloud slid over the moon, casting the village in darkness for several breaths.

He reached the watchtower. It was constantly manned now upon Haakon's insistence.

"Hey," he called up.

"Who goes there?"

A hooded figure with a bow slung over his cloak and a quiver of arrows on his back turned. "Hamish, that you?"

"Aye."

"It's me, Bryce."

"You see anyone go out?" Hamish asked his best friend.

"Aye, a while ago."

"Who was it?" His heart squeezed, knowing the answer already.

"A woman. Astrid, I think. Who else would tell me to fuck off when I warned her about the wolves?"

Hamish shook his head and frowned at the dark forest.

She was out there. Alone.

A little bit of his soul cracked. He hated to think of what turmoil she was in. It wasn't as if she couldn't take care of herself; he didn't doubt that. She was a force like no other. But to have upped and left the safety and security of Tillicoulty in the middle of the night, in darkness, in winter, she must have been broken, in despair, hurt.

And that didn't sit well with Hamish.

Even fiery, wicked, challenging women deserved to have their pain soothed.

Chapter Two

"MOTHER," HAMISH SAID, stepping into his family's small, round home.

Instantly, the warmth of the fire wrapped around him and the scent of herby broth filled his nose.

Lass let out a small bark, then jumped up and wound around his legs.

"Ah, Hamish." His mother, Fion, looked up, as did May, a friend and neighbor. "I thought you'd be in the council meeting with the king." She smiled, the wrinkles around her eyes deepening.

He reached for his thickest fur cape and threw it over his shoulders. "I was, but I have to do something." He grabbed a leather bag and a handful of dried meats and several apples.

"Where are you going?" his mother asked.

"Hunting. I have traps to check."

"In the middle of the night?" May asked with a frown.

"Aye, I forgot today, and I set some way downriver. Fish traps too."

"That is unlike you," his mother said. "To forget."

"I've had a lot on my mind." He paused and bit on his bottom lip. It did feel as though his mind were full. But it wasn't full of hunting and stalking; it was full of Astrid and her complex moods.

"I'm sure it could wait until daylight," his mother said. "Stay and have some broth."

"I have eaten. And this time of year, we must accept some things need to be done in the dark."

She set down the tunic she was sewing. "Well, be careful of the wolves. I heard them last night, so don't be long."

He went up to her and kissed her cheek. She smelled of lavender. "Don't worry. I'm more than capable of looking after myself in the forest, even if I come across wolves."

"I know, son, but—"

"But nothing. And I may be some time. I intend to set more traps, in the foothills of the mountains."

"But that is so far away."

"And will take me a while, so do not be concerned about me. I will return."

Her eyes flashed with worry.

"Stop it." He smiled. "God will be with me and I will return with meat."

She sighed and touched his cheek. "I will try not to worry. Be safe, my only son."

Hamish nodded at May then ducked out into the cold night again. He would set some traps, and hopefully, he'd get lucky. But his real prize would be to find Astrid and make sure she was well.

"Bryce," he called up to the watchtower. "Which way did she go?"

Through the darkness, and with the moon behind him like a halo, Bryce looked down, his broad shoulders silhouetted. "Toward the forest, east, the river track."

"You sure?"

"Aye." He paused. "Why? What are you doing?"

"I'm going after her."

"What? Are you soft in the head?"

"No, of course not."

"Then why would you go after that bad-tempered bitch?"

"Don't call her that." Hamish found his hackles rising. "She's unhappy here, that's all."

"She'd be *unhappy* anywhere on God's Earth, that one."

"She's…" He stopped himself from saying *complex, curious, intriguing*. Bryce wouldn't have understood. "She's the king's sister. We have a duty to make sure she is safe."

"So why doesn't the *king* go after her?"

"He is content in the Great House with his wife. I have no wife. I can track his sister and ensure her wellbeing. The king need not be concerned when he is otherwise engaged."

"Rather you than me," Bryce called. "If she finds out you've followed her, she'll use your guts as fishing lines."

He huffed. "I'll take that chance." He stepped through the gates beneath the watchtower. "But keep it to yourself, right."

"Keep what to myself?"

"That I've gone after her. I've told my mother I'm going hunting, heading east toward the mountains."

"If that's what you want me to do."

"Aye, it is. It's no one else's business what I do, but those bloody Vikings seem to think it is."

"You know I've always got your back," Bryce said gruffly. "Especially where *they* are concerned."

"Thanks, my friend."

Hamish walked out into the open and headed past the crops. The moon lit his way and it also revealed small, recent footprints. Bryce had been right. Astrid had headed east.

When Hamish reached the forest, the moonlight became fractured by the branches. His eyes had to adjust to the new darkness.

A rustling to his right had him pausing. It was a hare on a midnight prowl, its coat as white as the moon. Quickly, he dipped into his pocket, pulled out what he needed to make a trap, and set it.

Perhaps he'd be lucky when he returned to this spot later.

Continuing, he stayed alert to predators. An owl called in the distance. When the cool scent of the river reached his nose he left the track and went toward it.

He met the river at a meander along the shallow bank and slid down to the water's edge. It frothed and bubbled over rocks, rushing to get to the fall downstream. In the summer, it was a good place to fish for salmon. Right now, Hamish simply scooped up a handful and took a drink.

Straightening, he looked east at the snow-covered mountaintops peeking from the forest canopy. The foothills were good hunting ground and as soon as there was more light in the day, he would fulfill his promise to his mother and set traps there.

Right now, he had only one focus. Astrid.

He took to the track again and found her bootprints in the mud. Likely, it would snow again soon. The air had a nip to it and his fingers were icy.

He resumed his journey, heading toward Clam Bay. Was that where she'd gone? To the caves?

It would be a sensible thing to do. They would give shelter, and there was fresh water nearby as well as plentiful firewood. Plus, the bay always delivered food when the tide went out.

Astrid was no fool. If he knew one thing about her, it was that she had a sharp mind and was a quick thinker.

But what was she planning on doing in the cave all winter? Just sitting it out? Waiting for the weather to warm and the sea to calm? And if so, what was her intention after that? She couldn't make a boat on her own and sail away.

Could she?

The more he thought about it as he walked, the more he realized nothing she did would surprise him.

As the glistening sea came into view, so did the scent of smoke.

He'd been right. She was at the caves. And she'd made herself at home too, with fire, and if he wasn't mistaken, the scent of cooking clams.

A twist of nerves caught in his belly.

Now what?

She was clearly managing on her own, and quickly too. The best thing for him to do would be to turn around and head back to Tillicoulty. Leave her to it.

Suddenly, a long, low howl rang through the air. A lone wolf bemoaning its empty belly.

Hamish hated wolves. He'd had several encounters over the years and they had all been close calls.

And now, during the wolf moon, they were at their most dangerous. Desperate and daring, they roamed the forest searching for prey.

What Hamish really didn't want to happen was the wolves to set their sights on Astrid. A lone wolf, he had no doubt she could scare off, but a pack, emboldened by their numbers, sneaking up, prowling in the darkness, waiting for her guard to drop in the dead of the night…

No. Hamish couldn't bear the thought of that. He'd have to settle down to keep watch beside the big rock shaped like an otter. It stood to the left of the caves and looked down upon the beach.

He'd have a good view from there. Anything approaching, he'd see it first.

Mind made up, Hamish moved silently to the rock he and Kenna had used to climb over and jump off of when they'd been younger. Carefully pushing apart a patch of small yew shrubs, he found a sheltered spot that made a good vantage point.

He folded down and clasped his cape tighter against the bitter sea wind. His mouth watered at the smell of the cooking clams, even though he wasn't hungry. He imagined Astrid sitting on a flat stone near her fire carefully easing them from their shells. She'd no doubt wear a scowl, her movements brisk and efficient, and if her hair was loose, the light of the flames would catch in it, making it glow like copper and shine like the stars.

He shifted his weight and blew into his palms. If he were a braver man, he'd announce himself and sit with her.

But although Hamish considered himself a man of courage and morals, appearing at Astrid's side when she wanted to be alone... No, that wasn't bravery. That was stupidity.

WHEN ASTRID WOKE, her first thought was the fire. It had been the right priority, as it had almost gone out.

Quickly, she pushed from her makeshift bed, which had been surprisingly comfortable and warm, and stacked more kindling and a log onto the glowing embers.

Soon it was bursting into flames again, a satisfying crackle coming with it.

It was only then that she stood and stretched, her fingers not quite touching the cave roof. A few tendrils of ivy hung down from the entrance and a small rivulet of fresh water separated her new home from the beach, a gentle ripple of mountain overspill that went east to west at the top of the beach.

Peering outside and pushing her hair from her face, she studied the horizon. Another new day. And this one would be a better day because she wouldn't have to watch her brother fawning over his wife. Listen to the stupid village priest going on about his god. Or help teach the villagers how to hold a shield and defend against a sword— Haakon's insistence on daily battle lessons was boring. And what was she getting out of it? Nothing.

The sky was clear blue, not a cloud in sight, and it reflected in a relatively calm sea, giving the illusion of warm tranquility.

A sudden urge gripped her. To swim. At home in the north, the water was a death-defying cold, the lakes thick with ice. Even the waterfalls turned to ice—despite her divinity, the powerful water goddess, Sága, was unable to blow breath into it.

Pushing the ivy aside, Astrid stepped out onto the beach. It was fine, golden sand and shaped like a crescent moon. Several birds with orange beaks busied themselves by the rocks to her right, no doubt catching the small shellfish she'd dined on the night before. But to the left, the rocks gave way and the sand led a gateway to the gently ebbing waves.

The thought of feeling refreshed, cleansed, was too much to resist. After checking her fire was established, she took a drink of water then strode out onto the beach.

The briny air filled her nose and she watched a sea eagle circle then plunge its claws into the ocean, coming up with a wriggling fish.

It was good to know the water was bountiful.

Once at the narrow path to the ocean, she stopped and removed her sandy boots. She set them on a rock to protect them from being washed away, then added her pants to the pile.

The chill circled her buttocks and made the tiny hairs on her legs stand on end. She suppressed a shiver.

Next came her leather belt complete with dagger, twine, rune-stones, and flint, then her red, woolen tunic. Finally, she removed her breast binding and set that on the clothes.

Stepping into the shallowest wave, she held her face to the sky as the chill circled her ankles like two gripping hands.

"Oh, mighty Freya," she said to the sky. "All-Seeing Odin and powerful Thor, see me now, here, as your servant, and direct me on this, my most difficult path."

A raven cawed hoarsely behind her and she smiled, knowing Odin was indeed with her, seeing her, guiding her.

With her skin goosebumping, she walked into the sea. The waves were louder here and filled her ears. The horizon was flat and as she went deeper, the sand turned stony and sharp.

She pushed forward and swam several strokes. The cold stole her breath for a moment and it seeped between her legs, into her pussy, and pinched at her nipples. It was the stroke of a thousand tiny blades, leaving no part of her untouched.

"Oh, fuck," she muttered when she'd snatched in a breath.

Summoning strength, she struck out, swimming several fast paces, then she turned and went parallel to the shore until she felt a rock skimming her knee. She turned around, knowing how lethal the rocks in this bay were.

A few minutes later, she walked from the water, the cold, winter air like a slap to her naked body. She shivered, a full-body tremble that came from her core. Her hands and feet tingled and her shoulder muscles were tense.

But it felt good, and as she walked in a circle by her clothes, flapping her arms and air drying, she closed her eyes and enjoyed the cleanliness and the invigorating sense of being as free as the sea eagle.

When the worst of the drips were gone from her body and she'd squeezed the salty water from the ends of her hair, she slipped into her clothes again, bending to tighten her boots with stiff fingers and taking an extra moment to do up her belt.

It was then that she saw it.

Movement in her peripheral vision.

She had to force herself not to look too closely. Instincts told her it wasn't a wolf, nor even a deer.

Instincts told her it was a *someone*, not a something.

A fresh flush of heat warmed her cold body. It was angry heat. Fury. Indignation.

She'd been spied on.

The only question was by whom.

Forcing her steps to stay casual, she wandered back up the beach and into the cave. Once by the fire, she held out her palms to the heat and gritted her teeth, holding in a flurry of murderous promises.

Who the hell is it?

Haakon making sure she wasn't dead? No, he'd have shown himself and he certainly wouldn't have spied on her naked.

Orm? Perhaps. But would he care that she had stormed off into the night? Not really.

One of the crew? She doubted it. They had all been settled in with ale and food when she'd left them.

The priest. The fucking priest? *Ja*, it was probably him—slimy, old fool.

After a few minutes, she slipped from the cave, using the ivy as cover and moving tight against the edge of the rock face. Being careful not to stand on any driftwood or disturb any stones, she made her way to the track, keeping a watchful eye on the big, brown rock at the head of the beach.

Was her unwanted guest still there? She hoped so.

Gripping her dagger, she reached the rock and saw several disturbed yew shrubs.

With her heart thudding and her body fully warm again after her icy morning swim, she peered forward.

A fur cape, brown with a tasseled hood. One she recognized.

Of all the… It was Hamish MacCallum.

Chapter Three

HAMISH WOKE STIFF and thirsty. The rock had made for a poor pillow and the earth beneath him was cold.

He was about to slip back to the track and head for Tillicoulty when he heard logs being shifted and a fresh lick of smoke came from the cave.

Astrid was awake, and no doubt hungry. Perhaps now was the time to show himself and help her fish. The bay was always plentiful.

Just as he was about to stand, she appeared. For a moment, his heartbeat picked up and his breath seemed to catch in his throat. Her curled hair was loose and the strands caught the morning sunshine, as though actually soaking it up. He rubbed his fingertips on his palms, wishing he could feel it, discover its soft, silky texture. But of course he couldn't. She'd likely gut him if he tried.

Her attention was harnessed by a flock of oystercatchers searching for their breakfast. And then she ducked back into the cave, only to reappear seconds later.

She walked with purpose to the shoreline, taking the narrow path of sand between the rocks. A route Hamish knew well from his childhood.

Once there, she paused, then stooped and removed her boots.

His mouth dried and he swallowed tightly. What the hell was she doing?

But of course he knew. He'd done it himself enough times over the years, right there, in that exact spot.

She was going for a morning swim.

Next came her pants, exposing long, slender legs and pale buttocks. When she lifted her tunic up and off, he saw that her patch of female hair was pale and her abdomen flat.

"Oh, fuck," he muttered, his belly tightening and a stirring in his cock making him shift position.

He had to go. Get the hell out of there. If she ever found out he'd spied on her like this, he'd be a dead man.

He glanced right, wondering if he could get back to the path without her seeing. But right now, she was facing him and removing her breast binding.

"Dear Lord above," he muttered. Her slight breasts were white and pert, her nipples palest pink. As she moved, folding her tunic, her hair brushed over them.

His cock stiffened some more and now his mouth watered too. She was like a hot meal for a starving man, shelter in a storm, a boat when drowning. Everything a man could ever want.

As she stood in the shallowest ebb and flow of the waves with her back to him, Hamish knew he'd never seen anything more beautiful in his life and likely never would again. She was completely at ease with herself, delicate yet strong, wild yet somehow tamed by the natural world around her.

And then she walked into the water. His first thought was to go to her. It was dangerous this time of year when it had been so long since the summer sun had heated it. There were many tales in the village of people not being able to warm up again after a swim, or catch their breath once going under.

But he stayed exactly where he was, his breathing shallow and his cock tingling.

She pushed forward, a graceful glide into the water, and began to swim. A flame-haired selkie.

He glanced left and right, looking for danger. Occasionally, people spotted wolves of the sea. Huge, black-and-white whales that preyed on seals. He wouldn't put it past one to take a tasty human female.

She didn't swim for long and was soon getting out of the water, flapping her arms to dry in the stiff breeze.

Damn it, he was so hard, it hurt.

Again, he shifted his weight, trying to get comfortable. The yew to his right shook and a twig snapped underfoot.

He froze. Of all the luck, and when he'd been so careful.

But luckily, she hadn't noticed. She carried on getting dressed and then ambled back to the cave.

Good, he'd sit for a few minutes, let his erection abate, then head back to the village.

He closed his eyes and her image hovered there. Naked and beautiful. He was sure she'd lain with men before; the Vikings had different morals to Christians. Hamish had never touched a woman intimately. Not that he hadn't wanted to, it was just the teachings of God that he should wait until his wedding night.

What would it be like to couple with a woman like Astrid? A strange longing tugged his belly and his chest squeezed just at the thought.

Suddenly, there was movement behind him, the bush rustled, and then a cold, sharp blade pressed against his throat.

He stilled and his eyes widened, his hand on the handle of his own dagger. His cock deflated instantly.

"What in Odin's name do you think you're doing here?" Astrid hissed by his ear.

He swallowed tightly, his Adam's apple scraping on the blade she held flush with his neck.

"I was…" he managed. "Checking you were alive."

"Of course I'm alive." Her breath was hot by his ear. "You doubt that I have skills?"

"You don't know this land."

"Bullshit. You were spying on me."

"I wasn't." He didn't dare move. Her chest was pressed to his back and with one slide of her hand, it would be all over for him. "I promise I wasn't."

"Stand up."

"What?"

"You heard me."

Gingerly, he did as she'd instructed, unfolding to his full height and staring out at the beach. His bones ached and his feet and fingers were cold.

But standing had given him an advantage. He was a whole head taller than Astrid and that made it harder for her to keep the angle of her dagger at his neck.

"I should kill you for this. My brother likely will. He's the king, remember, and you've been peeking at his sister."

"I didn't know you were going to go swimming naked."

"Ah, so you admit it."

"Well, aye, of course I do. I was here. I witnessed your pleasure at becoming one with the sea."

She paused, as though not quite sure what to say.

He took advantage of the moment and carefully turned to face her. The blade stayed up against his neck.

Her furious glare was enough to freeze a midsummer stream and her lips were a tight flat line. There was a tiny rise of color on her cheeks, like two small crab apples in the sunshine.

"I'm sorry," he said. "I was just leaving."

"It's too late for apologies." Her blade still pressed against his flesh.

"There is nothing more I can offer you than that."

"Too damn right there isn't." She kind of snarled and in that moment, she reminded him of a wildcat.

"So I'll go." He flicked his eyes at the track.

"I don't think so."

A madness crossed over her irises. It was intent and lethal and Hamish couldn't have ignored it if he'd wanted to. He had to do something in the name of self-preservation.

He took a step back and swiped at the arm that held the dagger, knocking it from his throat.

She let out a yelp of fury and swung it back toward him on a lethal journey to his chest.

Quickly, he sidestepped around her, flattening the yews further and putting distance between himself and the blade.

But she was fast and nimble and she rounded on him again.

This time, she tore his cape, but the blade's drag on the thick material caused her to drop the dagger.

She huffed and stooped, but Hamish kicked it away and then grabbed her upper arms.

"Get the hell off me," she yelled, wriggling wildly, like a fish caught on a hook.

"Stop it. I mean you no harm."

"You are a peeping, Christian idiot," she said, her hair bouncing around her face. "Don't touch me."

Still, he gripped her.

But suddenly, she dropped her body weight and his grip slackened. She rammed her boot at his shin and he stumbled forward. A huge, hard shove in his back sent him sprawling onto the track, his nose planting in mud.

A strange banshee scream filled his ears, then a weight landed on him, knees and fists rained down on his body over and over.

"Jesus Christ," he gasped as he tried to turn.

She bashed his head with the heel of her hand, his nose dipping into the mud once more.

"Urgh!" He spluttered. "Could you just…"

"You asshole." She slapped him around the head again then went for a kidney punch.

Luckily, his thick cloak broke the impact, but still, he grunted in discomfort.

"I've thought you were a pathetic, little baby since the minute I saw you," she shouted breathlessly as she continued to rain thumps onto his shoulders. "I should cut your throat just for existing and then chop off your dick and feed it to you so everyone can see what a cocksucker you are."

In the name of the Lord, this woman was a blaspheming banshee. He had to stop this.

"Enough." Hamish frowned and summoned his strength. It was clear she wasn't going to burn herself out and if she got hold of that dagger again, he was done for.

He heaved over, twisting so that he was facing her, then gripped her wildly flailing wrists and surged upward. Within a second, she was on her back, her slight weight no match for his strength and size, and her crown dipping into the mud where his nose had just been.

She let out a feral cry of fury and glared at him with eyes full of hate as she kicked and struggled.

"Will you just..." he managed as he set his legs on either side of her hips and dragged her arms above her head. He huffed with the effort. She might have been small, but she was as slippery as a snake.

"Get off me!" she shouted again. "You'll... You'll hang for this. I'll see that you do. The ravens will be feasting on your eyeballs before sundown."

"Astrid!" A muddy drip fell from his nose and landed on her cheek. "Would you just stop this? I'm sorry. I'm really sorry I saw you."

She let out a strangled scream and bucked upward as though hoping to knock him off.

He tightened his hold on her wrists. Her bones were small and delicate and her body petite beneath his. "I don't want to hurt you."

"Just spy on me and play with your cock, right." Her teeth gritted and her eyes narrowed. "Make yourself come as you watch me swim without clothes. Huh?"

"What? No, why would I do that?"

"Because you're a man."

"Not *that* kind of man. I was making sure you were safe. I sat all night here watching for wolves. They're around these parts. They've come down from the mountains and they are hungry and brave."

She stilled, though her breaths were coming hard and fast, her chest rising and falling and her nostrils flaring. "You were here all night?"

"Aye."

"That just makes you sly too." She clamped her lips together and continued to glare up at him.

"For caring? That makes me sly? Your brothers and friends weren't going to check on you."

"I don't need checking on. I told you. I can look after myself. I have the skills to survive for as long as I want to on my own."

"I know, I understand, but…"

"'But'?"

Hamish hesitated, then, "I wanted to see if you were all right. I was worried that your feelings might be hurt."

"'Worried,'" she spat. "Worried, about my feelings. Who in the name of Odin told you it was *your* job to worry about any part of me, let alone my feelings? I don't need you worrying. I don't need you following me. I don't need—"

"I get it." He lowered his face to hers. Her warm breath touched his cheek and the salty scent of the ocean that lingered on her skin filled his nose. "I get that you don't need me, and that's fine. Absolutely fine."

Her pupils were so wide and dark, he felt like he could see right into her soul. But that didn't make it any easier to understand her.

"So I'll go," he said, quieter now that she was still and appeared to be listening to him. "I'll go and leave you alone so you can do whatever it is you think you're going to do next. Whatever mad plan you have in that pretty, wee head of yours."

"*Ja*, go. Get off me."

"Are you going to grab your dagger and stab me the minute I let go?" He raised his eyebrows at her.

"That's for me to know and you to find out." She raised one eyebrow.

"Ah. I guess I'll have to trust in the Lord that you aren't the murderous wildcat you'd have everyone believe you are."

"'Murderous wildcat.' Why, you..."

Hamish chuckled and released her wrists.

Instantly, she scooted up and away from him, springing to her feet. She glanced at her dagger on the other side of the rock. "You said you were going." She swiped at a drip of mud on her cheek. Several leaves were stuck in her hair and there was a dark patch of dirt over her ear.

He had to stop himself from stepping up to her and removing the leaves. Instead, he took a pace backward. "I am."

"Good."

He nodded once, straightened his cloak, and turned.

"And I do not have a 'pretty, wee head'!" she yelled just before the forest shadows ate him up. "So don't you dare say anything stupid like that again."

"I thought you didn't want to see me again." He kept on walking.

She let out a strangled, growling sound and he was sure she'd stomped her foot onto the ground. "I don't. Go. Stay away."

Hamish chuckled quietly and ducked into the forest.

"I mean it! Don't come back! You bloody idiot."

Not go back? Not see her again? That wasn't going to happen. There was something about Astrid that had piqued his interest, sparked his desires in a way nothing or no one had before.

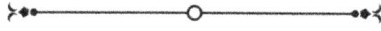

Chapter Four

ASTRID SLAMMED HER hands onto her hips and watched Hamish stride into the forest. His fur cloak was filthy, as was his hood and the back of his head. She was still breathing hard and she was hot, her heart thudding.

How dare he follow her? Secretly watch over her? *Spy* on her when she was naked?

He was even more annoying than her brother Orm and even more infuriating than Haakon when he was being overprotective.

"I mean it. Don't come back!" she shouted after him, flicking her hand in his direction. "You bloody idiot."

But Hamish was gone and he didn't reply.

She gave in to the urge to stomp her foot on the ground for a second time. "Of all the…" She turned and found her dagger, sliding it into her belt. She then jumped up onto the rock, slammed her hands onto her hips, and stared out to sea. "Odin, if you send a boat my way, I swear I will swim to it and row with all my strength back to the north and away from these foolish Christians with their childish ways."

The sea eagle swooped again, successfully catching another fish—a flash of silver in its talons. Her stomach rumbled and she wondered how easily she could catch a fish from one of the rocks.

Jumping down to the ground, she headed back to her cave, collecting several pieces of driftwood on the way. She'd need a good pile if the snow came again.

"Food is what I need first." She grabbed a crust of bread from her sack of supplies, took a bite, then set about making a hook with bait. With luck, the fish would be hungry too and she'd get breakfast.

AN HOUR LATER, Astrid had a good pile of dry wood and her fishing line was set. She set a pot of water over the fire, then, as it warmed, she drank ale. Her face was muddy and there was a patch of hair that also needed cleaning.

Annoying, when she'd been fresh from the sea not so long ago.

Another reason Hamish was a pain in the rear.

Her stomach rumbled again and after cleaning herself, she wandered down the beach, disturbing the flock of beachcombing birds who'd made their way closer to her end. They took off in a flap and panic, squawking their displeasure.

But her line was empty, and she frowned at the sea eagle circling. He was scaring her catch away.

Resentment took hold; it seeded, germinated, and bloomed. Not just resentment at the sea eagle, but bitterness for Ravn, Haakon, Hamish...even her mother for leaving her alone with a family of bossy, self-righteous men. Her father had said Astrid was a knotted soul and he was right, for at this moment, she felt as though the very sinews of her body had been twisted and tightened into hard, thick lumps that she couldn't undo.

She opened her mouth and yelled at the sea, trying to let go of the hurt. It was like clutching burning pieces of wood that she wanted to drop. Every time she'd been told she wasn't big enough because she was a girl, not strong enough, fast enough because she was a girl, was a hot scar etched in her memory and she wanted them all to go away.

And why hadn't she been considered for her father's crown? She would have made an excellent queen for the people of Drangar and her father knew it...yet he had never even mentioned it.

Again, because she was a girl.

She yelled some more, a deep bellow that used up every drop of air in her lungs. She imagined the sound floating up to the highest realm. Surely, the gods would see her pain and her desperation at being stuck here on a foreign beach in a foreign land, and they'd help her.

When the cry had finally left her throat she dashed at the tears that had spilled from her eyes and bent double. She was all alone. That was what she'd wanted when she'd stormed from the Great House the night before. Solitude was at least one thing to be grateful for.

As were the shellfish all around her. They might not have been her favorite—she hated the grains of sand that always sneaked into her mouth—and she needed to eat a lot to fill her belly, but at least there was food.

She began to collect the little shells. She found a crab too, and added him to her pouch.

When she had gathered enough for a meal, along with a handful of seaweed, she wandered back up the beach with a furrow on her forehead. She wasn't looking forward to her gritty breakfast. She really should have planned better when she'd loaded her sack.

She ducked through the ivy tendrils and into the cave then sat on a rock beside her fire. The air was cold and she warmed her palms as water boiled.

Suddenly, there was movement.

"Who goes there?" She jumped up, dagger at the ready. Perhaps it wasn't a *who* but a *what*.

Nothing.

"Show yourself." Her heart thudded as a rush of preparedness tensed her muscles, ready for the fight.

"It's me."

"Hamish?" She stepped to the entrance as he appeared in it.

His shoulders were wide, his hair tousled, and in his hand a fat, white hare hung limply. It had been gutted and skinned.

"I told you to stay away. Do you not understand your own language?"

He ignored her. "I set a trap on my way here yesterday, got lucky, so thought I'd drop it off for you. Not many hares on the beach."

"I am about to go and set—"

"Of course you are and no doubt you'll catch many dinners. But for now, I've got this one. Want it?"

"Don't you want it?" Why was he being generous like this? What did he want?

"Aye, I want some of it. I'm starving, and it was a long, cold night."

Uninvited, he stepped in, his big boots crunching on the ground as he seemed to fill up so much of her space with his presence.

Her stomach rumbled and she added an extra log to the fire then hunted in her small log store for sticks to use as a spit.

He watched her silently, as though not wanting to say the wrong thing. Which was wise of him. If she hadn't been so unexcited about eating the cockles and a single small crab, she would have chased him away.

"Here." She passed him a long stick.

"Thanks." He sat on a rock with his back to the wall and set about preparing the hare for cooking.

Astrid sat opposite, leaning forward, her forearms on her thighs as she looked out to sea.

She hoped he hadn't heard her screaming her frustration. That would be embarrassing.

"Snow is coming," he said.

"The sky is clear." She rolled her eyes.

"Not over the mountains. It is heavy and dark and it always blows in this way before spring."

She said nothing. Snow would make life harder, but it didn't scare her.

"Shouldn't take too long," Hamish said, balancing the hare over the heat.

She shrugged.

"Is that ale?" he asked, nodding at her bottle.

"*Ja.*"

"Can I have some?"

"If you must."

"I must." He chuckled and took a swig before passing it to her and wiping the back of his hand over his mouth. He wore a small, stone cross around his neck. It had a hole in the top and was strung with thin, brown leather.

Astrid also drank then set the ale back on the makeshift shelf. "So tell me," she said, picking up a handful of small pebbles and rolling them in her palm, "how hard was your cock when you watched me strip naked?"

"What?" His eyes widened.

"You understood the question." She tossed a stone at him, hitting him on the chest. It bounced to the ground. "Don't play dumb."

"Hey." He frowned.

"On a scale of one to ten," she said, tipping her head and jangling the stones. "When you first saw my tits, how hard were you?"

"I… I wasn't. Jesus, Astrid, why would you ask me that?"

"'Cause I'm curious."

"Well, don't be."

She threw another stone at him. This time, it hit him on his shoulder.

"Stop that."

"So tell me how hard you were and then I'll stop. Did your cock go to half hardness or full hardness when I walked into the sea and you saw my ass?"

His lips pressed into a tight line.

She threw another stone, enjoying seeing a rise of color blooming on his pale cheeks.

He glared at the stone as it landed on the ground.

"I reckon," she said, "that you had a full-on boner in your pants. That all the blood from your head went to it and made you dizzy."

"I did not."

She raised her eyebrows. "So it was just a semi?"

"It was nothing. Shut the fuck up."

She grinned and threw another stone, aiming for his chin.

He batted it away and it bounced off the cave wall. "Will you stop that?"

"What? Asking you about your cock or throwing stones?"

"Both." He scowled at her and leaned forward to adjust the hare.

"Why? Because it's true, you got hard...or maybe you made yourself come when you watched me. Did you do that? Grunt with pleasure and jack yourself off?"

"I did no such thing." His cheeks were getting pinker.

"Why not? Most men would. Or don't you think I'm pretty?" She threw a stone at his face, but he caught it. "Am I ugly to you?"

"I didn't do that...jack myself off...because it would be a sin in the eyes of God."

"What? To make yourself come?" This surprised her. What kind of God didn't approve of pleasure?

"It would be disrespectful to you." He leaned back and folded his arms, eyeing the small stone she was flipping from one hand to the other. "That is why it would be a sin."

"'Disrespectful'?"

"Aye, and if I had, I wouldn't be able to sit here, look you in the eye, and say...say that I didn't masturbate as I spied on you. I speak my truth."

She hesitated, then, "I believe you."

"I'm glad you do, but if you didn't, then it wouldn't matter because God knows the truth."

"If your god knows the truth, if he is all-seeing, he'll notice, like I have, that you haven't denied getting hard." She threw the last stone at him. "Have you?"

He caught it with a snatch of his hand.

"So you *did* get hard. Your cock approved of my nakedness." She laughed. "Didn't it?"

"If you're so smart, then tell me what you think." He leaned forward, dropping the stone to the ground as he studied her.

"I think you wanted to look away but couldn't help yourself. I think your cock got hard and your mouth got dry. Your heart, it beat faster and your breaths quickened. I think that you wondered what it would be like to touch me, to bend me over and sink your cock into my hot, tight pussy. That's what *I* think."

He nodded slowly and a smile spread on his lips. "You have a filthy mind, you know that."

"So do you."

"You can't possibly know what I think."

"You're a man. I've been surrounded by men all my life. They think with their cocks, and when they're not thinking of sex they're thinking of power, revenge, and war."

A line appeared between his eyebrows. "You have a low opinion of men."

"Garnered from experience."

"Well, we are always learning, so maybe that opinion will change with time."

"You think you're so smart, Hamish." She crossed her legs and jabbed her boot into the air.

"I don't pretend to be smart, but I do know a few things about myself."

"Which are?" She huffed. Why was she even interested?

"I value peace, loyalty, faith, and compassion. I don't seek war or revenge and I have never thought with my cock."

"Of course you have thought with your cock. Every man has." This was a truth she knew as well as day turned to night.

"Even one who is a virgin?" He stared at her, unblinking. His green eyes flashed in the shadows. "Does a virgin think with his cock?"

"What?" He had to have been lying. Him...a grown man...a virgin.

"You understood the question. Don't play dumb, Astrid."

She folded her arms tightly. "You are *not* a virgin."

"Why wouldn't I be?" He looked as though he were holding in a grin.

"Because... Because." She flicked her hand at him. "You're a man, of, what... twenty-five summers at least and..."

"And?"

"Well, you're not ugly. There must be at least one village woman who would spread her legs for you."

He laughed, a soft, deep sound. "'Haps, but God instructs us to wait until our wedding night. Look at Haakon and my sister. Kenna was a virgin when they wed, as is our Christian way."

Astrid frowned. So it was the same for both men and women in this strange land? How awful, how dreary, for them all.

"You don't understand our ways," he said, poking at the embers then adding another log to the fire. "But that's not a problem for me."

"I understand pleasure. I love sex. During the long, dark winter months, it staves off boredom and keeps me warm. It's Freya's will that lust and longing must not be denied. It can make you sick if you do deny yourself."

"'Lust and longing.'" He nodded slowly and bit on his bottom lip.

A strange, little kernel of interest popped in her belly. It had been some time since she'd indulged in sweaty, spontaneous sex. Perhaps it would be fun to show Hamish what he'd been missing out on. She was sure he had a great body under those thick clothes and it might be nice to watch him discover just how good she could make him feel. See those pink cheeks flush some more and watch his mouth hang slack as bliss took him. "You must have felt lust."

"I said I was a virgin, not a monk." He laughed. "Of course I have felt lust. Of course I have wanted to bed pretty women. But I also have restraint and self-control."

"I think it's weird." She shrugged nonchalantly. "You're weird."

"That's your opinion." He also shrugged. "Because I'm not defined by what other people think of me or my choices."

"So what does define you?" She glanced outside. The sky was darkening, as he'd said it would.

"What defines me?" He twisted his lips as though thinking deeply. "I guess my love for my family and God. My ability to survive—"

"Huh, you wouldn't survive one day in the true north."

He nodded slowly. "Tell me about it."

She pointed out to the sea. The waves were whipping up, white curls of froth rolling into one another. "The sun doesn't come up for many weeks. There's barely a sliver of light on the horizon, though in the black sky, great ribbons of green and gold dance as the gods practice their sword fighting. The window each summer for growing crops is short and if the rains come and wash the seeds away, flooding the field, the village goes hungry. That is a fact. The soil is poor, the cliffs steep, and the bears—I haven't seen evidence of any here—are always hungry and angry."

"We have bears here." He fiddled with the roasting hare. "But they are shy. They stay in the depths of the forest."

She huffed. "You are lucky."

"So tell me what the true North bears are like."

"They are huge, as big as the tallest man when they rear up. And their jaws are colossal, their teeth sharp, and—"

"Surely, you can outrun something that heavy."

"No." She pushed back a memory of being chased by a bear she and Orm had disturbed. "They are fast, very fast, and they can climb trees too. Their claws are like curved knives to grip into trunks."

"I wouldn't like to meet one without my bow and arrow."

"Which would do you no good. They have thick fur and thicker skin. A dagger to the heart is the only way to save yourself and by then, you would be so close, the creature would bite your head off."

He blew out a breath and laughed almost nervously. "Well, I am glad I was born here, where bears are not a problem."

"True, but you have many problems here, some you can see, some you cannot." She stared out to sea again. Why did she care that Tillicoulty would soon be attacked? Why did she care that Hamish had never enjoyed a night of sex?

She didn't. No. She really couldn't give an owl's hoot about any of it.

Chapter Five

"WHAT'S THAT?" HAMISH asked, suddenly pointing at the waves.

"Nothing." Astrid frowned.

"Aye, it is something. Something is washing up on the tide." He stood and strode to the entrance of the cave.

Astrid glanced at the cooking hare. It smelled good.

"Look!" Hamish stepped from the cave. "It's wood and... Is that a sail?"

She rushed to his side. The wind instantly whipped her hair up around her face and she shoved it behind her ears and pulled up her hood. "I think...I think it might be our sail, finally come ashore."

"And wood, from the hull of your boat. We should get it before the snowstorm hits. It will be useful to us."

"To me. Useful to *me*." She frowned up at him then took off at a run over the beach, her feet sinking into the soft sand. Glancing behind herself, she spotted the steely, fat clouds, and went faster.

Hamish was quickly at her side. "You grab the sail. I'll pull the wood up to the cave."

"It will be too wet to burn."

"Aye, but 'haps I can use it to make the cave more weatherproof for you."

She watched him stoop in the shallow waves and slide several dark planks of wood over each other. They were indeed from a boat, though whether or not it was theirs, she didn't know.

Quickly, she grabbed the red sail. It still had two ropes attached, though the ends were frayed. The material also had a long slit in it, almost ripping it in two. But when she had so little it would be precious.

She balled it up, gathering an annoying amount of sand and several shelves, then turned and rushed up the beach. A few fat snowflakes fell in front of her. Day had turned to night.

When she'd dumped the sail in the cave, she turned and rushed to help Hamish.

But he didn't need help. He had several heavy planks over his shoulder and was stomping toward her with his head stooped against the bitter wind and the falling snow.

He reached her quickly and dumped his load just outside of the cave. "Like this," he said, beginning to stack the planks on their ends, shoving the tips into the foliage that hung down. "So you can keep more heat in."

The wind had caught his hood, but he didn't seem to notice and continued with his task, lugging the heavy wood upward as though it were as light as a spring branch.

For a moment, Astrid admired his strength and sense of purpose, but then he irritated her and she grabbed the sail up again and shook it out.

The rapidly approaching storm tried to grab it from her, almost pulling it from her grip as the wet material flacked wildly.

"Good," Hamish said, reaching for the opposite end. "Now we'll put it inside, against this wood. It will soon dry and it will give us a wall at the end of the cave.

"It will be dark."

"We have fire and candles."

"*I* have fire and candles." She moved inside the cave with him. "But it will smoke us out."

"There'll be enough of a gap." Snowflakes clung to his red hair and peppered his shoulders. His eyes flashed with determination. "I promise, this will be a good thing."

Is he *a good thing?*

Should she be glad he'd followed her?

No. He was a pain in the ass. Bossy, at that. And a virgin. Well, she just didn't believe him about that.

An hour later, the storm was in full swing. The snow wasn't falling downward; it was set in spirals, Thor sending it in gusty swirls that had made Astrid dizzy when she'd peered around the sail to look out.

Hamish sat by the fire, the shadows dancing on his face as he ate his fill of the hare, crab and cockles. He had a silvery scar on the outer edge of his right eye. It was curved, like a crescent moon. A fraction to the left and he'd have lost his vision due to whatever it was that had wounded him.

"Your hair is messy," she said to him. "Do you never cut it?"

"My hair." His eyebrows lifted in surprise at the sudden criticism and he stopped chewing. "You are concerned about my hair?"

"I am not *concerned*—I am simply pointing it out. Vikings have hairstyles; they take more pride than you do in their appearance."

He ran his hand over his curly hair, pushing it back from his face. "And you think I should have a hairstyle?"

"*Ja.*" She shrugged. "It would be more practical if it was out of your face."

He kind of laughed. "I guess. I'll chop it off, then."

"No, no, don't chop it off. Plait it or something."

"'Plait it'?" He popped a chunk of meat into his mouth. "That's not for me."

"Why not?"

"I can't plait." He shrugged. "I'll have to cut it off if you think it's a hindrance."

"I'll plait it for you." She tossed a bit of gristle onto the fire and wiped her hands on her pants. "Turn around."

"What? You want to plait it now?"

"Nothing else to do."

He shrugged and shifted on the rock, gnawing on bone.

Astrid stood behind him. His hair matched the glowing embers. It was the only time she'd seen anyone with hair color that matched hers. Was it a sign from the goddess Freya that they had been destined to meet? Was it an omen that he'd appear with food and his strong muscles when she'd needed it? Not that she wouldn't have survived. He'd just made it easier...for now.

"When are you going back to the village?" she asked, sliding her fingers through the soft strands.

"When do you want me to?"

"Now." She frowned at him. "If you must know."

"The storm is harsh. Your god Thor must want me to stay here with you." He kind of chuckled.

"Why would you say that?" She tugged the hair over his right ear a little harsher than she'd planned to.

"Ouch." Again, he chuckled. "I'm just trying to understand how you think?"

"Well, don't."

He sat quietly.

Astrid set to work twisting his hair and tying the ends with little strips of fiber from the sail rope. The cave was warming up, her belly was full, and she started to relax a little and thought of how she'd learned to plait male hair this way on her father.

"Your brother," Hamish said, when he'd finished eating.

"Which one?"

"Haakon."

"What about him?"

"It was always his ambition to be king? A king. Anywhere?"

"I guess so." She worked her fingers nimbly, her knuckles brushing his warm nape.

"Why?"

"It is his destiny. It is the path set out for him by the gods. Would you not like that path for yourself?"

"I could have claimed the title of village leader from my father, had I wanted."

"But you didn't want?"

"No, and he was happy to continue, even though his body pains him in his old age."

"But why would you refuse power?" Didn't all men desire control and influence and harbor the need to rule?

"'Power'?" He paused as she gently retrieved a strand of hair from in front of his ear and pulled it back. "Power is not something I want."

"I thought every man wanted it."

"The head that wears the crown never sleeps easy. There is always someone waiting to steal it, to kill and maim for it. I wish for a simpler life."

"I understand what you mean." She finished the last plait and gathered them at the base of his crown. "I dislike the complication other people bring to my table. Even family at times." She paused. "I have finished."

He touched the top of his head, feeling over the rows of tight hair. Already, some of it was springing free. Astrid wasn't sure how long the curls would stay controlled. He stood and turned. "I'm sure, as you said, this will be very practical." He took a step closer to her, his concentration firmly on her face. "Thank you."

She backed up until her shoulders hit the cave wall. He looked different with his hair drawn from his face. His features were more angular, his green eyes more striking, and he also looked older, more mature...more handsome.

"Do you really want me to leave?" he asked quietly as he set one hand on the rock beside her left ear. "Now?"

She stared up at him. "Would you if I asked?"

"Of course. I wouldn't want to be somewhere I'm not wanted."

"You're not wanted. I left Tillicoulty to be alone."

"I'm not wanted?" He raised his eyebrows and put his other hand on the wall, blocking her in with his wide torso.

"No." For a moment, she thought about kneeing him in the balls, but then she realized his body heat was quite welcome and he smelled of not just the fire smoke, but also the pine forest.

"Are you sure about that, Astrid?" His voice was a low murmur. "Do you hate me that much?"

"It's… It's not *you* I hate, even though you are a Christian."

He raised his eyebrows. "So tell me what you hate."

"Why?"

"I want to understand why you're so angry at the world, even when you have so much."

"'Have so much'? What do I have?" Her heart rate picked up, a mixture of irritation and anticipation.

"You have…" He tipped his head, his gaze roaming her face. "You have so many skills, much knowledge, experience, and wisdom. You have traveled. You can fight and trap and swim and run. You love your gods fiercely and I admire that. I admire *you*."

"Those things are not possessions."

"Wealth is not about material possessions. It is about love." He smiled, just a little. "When you love you are rich and will be in this life and the next."

"What do you know of the next life?" She balled her hands into fists, ready to push him away. Who did he think he was, hemming her in like this and saying such things about her?

"I know it's a place where you meet with God, the Holy Father, and with all the people you love who have left before you."

"The people you love who are dead?"

"Aye."

She was watching his mouth moving as he spoke. It was so close to hers. She could see the pale stubble over his top lip. "I will also see the people I love when I reach Valhalla and feast with the gods." And she was looking forward to seeing her sweet, gentle mother again. She thought of it often with warm anticipation.

"So we are not so different, then, with what we believe."

She frowned. "We are very different."

His eyes narrowed slightly and he pressed his lips together as though holding in words.

Which irritated her. "Oh, shut up," she said, pushing at his hard chest and ducking to the right. "You talk shit, you know that."

He gave a tight, little laugh. "For everything, there is a season, Astrid."

"What does that mean?"

"'Haps this is the season for you to decide what you really want out of your mortal life."

"What I really want is to go back to Drangar. I want to see my father. He is the only man I've ever loved or ever will love."

"Then I think you have decided already what you want to do."

"*Ja*, I have. But before I do it…" She pointed at the bed. "I wish to sleep."

"Sleep, aye. I will keep the fire stoked. Keep the cave warm."

She paused and a wicked idea popped into her head. "Unless you want to lie with me. I could teach your virgin cock a thing or two. Finally show you the pleasure of a wet cunny."

He crossed his arms, rocked back on his heels, and nodded slowly. "Tempting, aye, very tempting."

"So? It's not every day a Princess of Drangar invites you to her bed. What will you choose, boy?"

Was he going to do it? She'd only been joking. But if he said *yes*… Well, she'd do it. Definitely. It would pass the time until the storm blew away and she was well overdue a few orgasms.

"I think I'll pass on this occasion. But don't worry, I'll sit here and watch out for wolves." Hamish sat and picked up one of the last hunks of meat. "You have a good sleep now, Astrid. I wish you sweet dreams."

"Huh, I only ever dream of battles and bears," she snapped as she crawled onto the soft bed area strewn with furs. "If you must know." She dropped down and tucked herself into a ball. She needed sleep, a solid, dark sleep that would restore her energy. And if Hamish was going to keep watch, it would be all the sounder.

He had uses, that much was clear.

Chapter Six

HAMISH WOKE WITH a stiff neck. He'd slept with his back against the damp cave wall. If Astrid's dreams had been about battles and bears, his had been about the ocean—a sea voyage on tempestuous water that was as calm as a pond one minute, then crashing around him in a violent rage the next.

"The storm has passed." Astrid was at the cave entrance peering around the sail.

The fire burst back to life; she'd obviously just thrown a log onto it.

He stretched his arms over his head and yawned. "Good. They can often go on for days."

"Thor has been benevolent. We must make a sacrifice to give thanks."

"Aye, we should."

"Don't mock me." She scowled at him. "I know you don't believe in my ways."

"But I believe in *you*." He smiled at her angry, little face. "And so I respect your ways."

"You might say that, but you'd like to see me changed to Christian the way your sister had Haakon changed." She gestured to his cross.

"Maybe you will when the time is right." God was merciful and welcoming, he knew that much.

"It never will be. Don't be such a fool."

Hamish shrugged and went to run his hand through his hair but then remembered the braids. He sighed. "Shall we break our fast? What do we have to eat?"

"There is some stale bread there and have some ale, but not all of it."

"Quite the feast."

She slipped from the cave, a flash of bright daylight bursting into the darkness for a split second.

Hamish tore off a piece of bread and swigged ale. Perhaps his dream about the volatile, unpredictable ocean had really been about Astrid and her changing, erratic moods. One moment, she was tenderly plaiting his hair, seeming to play with the strands, brushing his nape, his ear, the side of his cheek. Then she was telling him she wished he weren't there yet looking at him as though she wanted him to kiss her.

And when she'd offered him her body from the sultry shadows of the cave—the chance to finally rid himself of his virginity—it had taken a lot of willpower to refuse her. No one had ever tempted him as much as her, and he'd harnessed every morsel of self-control to obey his beliefs, and the promise he'd made to his mother.

Most of his friends in the village had long since given up trying to maintain celibacy, and they spoke of pleasure and ecstasy in hushed whispers and hoped their women wouldn't get pregnant before they asked for their hands in marriage.

"*I could teach your virgin cock a thing or two. Finally show you the pleasure of a wet cunny.*"

Her words came back to him in a flurry of sensuality. Heat instantly grew in his groin and he glanced at the pile of furs and blankets she'd slept on at the back of the cave. A candle still burned on a rocky incline. It was getting low.

He stepped over to it and blew out the flame. As he rested his hand on a white fur, he was sure her body heat still lingered there, soaking into his palm.

"Fuck," he muttered. "Don't let her do this to you. Not her. Not her of all the people in the world."

He stood straight and closed his eyes. Her face hovered there. Astrid had been sneaking her way into his brain from the moment he'd met her. Invading his thoughts and now his dreams too, or so it seemed.

And how had he found himself holed up with her in Clam Bay in the middle of winter?

She was a woman he shouldn't want—a heathen, bad tempered, crude of mouth—yet he couldn't help what he wanted.

And, it seemed, that was her.

"Hey, idiot Christian boy. Get your ass out here and show me what you've got."

He scowled at the sail then tightened his cloak and stepped outside.

The sun dazzled. It was a perfect blue-skied winter day. For a moment, he paused and let his eyes adjust.

"Over here," Astrid called.

He looked to his right. There was a light sprinkle of snow on the beach, though the fir trees beyond were heavy with it. The oyster-catchers that lived in the bay were at the far end, their orange beaks flashing in the sun. Astrid stood with two thick pieces of driftwood she appeared to have roughly fashioned into swords.

"What do you want?" he asked, marching toward her, his boots crunching on the icy ground.

"Come fight me."

"What? Why?"

"For practice." As he got closer, she tossed one of the wooden swords at him.

He caught it and spun it in his hand, testing the weight. "Why do you need to practice? I thought you could fight well already."

"I can. I want to see if *you* can."

"You doubt me?"

"Maybe I just want a good saga to tell my children one day. How I beat the flame-haired Lothlender into submission with a wooden sword."

"I'm sure you already have many sagas for your future children."

"I always need more." She raised her sword and set her feet apart. She'd discarded her cloak and her slender arms were strong beneath the sleeves of her tunic.

Hamish had to admire the glint of confidence in her blue eyes. Despite him being a head taller and likely the weight of a heavy lamb more, she appeared sure of her victory.

"If it's what you want," he said, also raising his sword.

She bobbed from one foot to the other then skipped to the right, the left, and then behind him.

He turned and blocked a jab to his left kidney.

"I have just woken up," he said gruffly.

"And would that be an excuse to your enemy who had crept up to the cave in the night?"

He huffed. She had a point.

He lifted his sword again and followed her round in a circle as she dodged and ducked. It was clear she used her nimbleness to her advantage.

To their right, a raven cawed.

"See?" she said. "Odin himself is seeing us, cheering me on. He knows his faithful ones and his true warriors."

"How is he seeing you?"

"He gave up his eye to the ravens, for knowledge, so that he would always know what his loyal servants are doing. It is this way he can converse with the other gods and map our destinies, and send the Valkyrie when our time comes in battle."

She lunged for him and he narrowly avoided the tip of her sword stabbing his groin.

"Who are these Valkyrie?" he asked.

She was grinning; she knew she'd nearly got him. "They are beautiful maidens sent by Freya, the Goddess of Love, Sex, War, Magic, and Beauty, to take the fallen to the next realm."

"You have a goddess for sex?"

"Of course. I told you: it's important." She winked. "And fun. Not that you would know."

He lifted his sword and swung it in her direction.

She laughed. "Is that all you have?"

"I don't want to hurt you."

"You won't." She swung at his head and he ducked and blocked. "You *can't* hurt me." She laughed and skipped backward, spinning a circle with her sword aloft.

His stomach grumbled and his bladder reminded him he needed to pee. It was time to draw this game to an end.

He swiped at her upper arm.

She blocked him then went for his head.

He stopped the contact and stepped up close, swiping her feet from under her with one swift movement.

She hit the sand with a *whump*, her hair falling forward as she landed on her hands and knees. Her sword skittered out of reach.

"You ass!" She spun and kicked out, taking both his feet.

He fell forward, landing next to her on the hard, cold sand and his sword flying to the right. Air was knocked from his lungs and his cheek scratched on the gritty surface.

Astrid was up in a second, springing to her feet like a little cat. "I win."

"How do you figure that?" He twisted and stared up at her.

The sun was directly behind her, spilling through her red hair and giving her a strange, bloody-orange halo.

"You're down, I'm up. If I had a knife or a real sword, I could kill you." She set her hands on her hips and gave him a cocky grin.

"You think?"

"*Ja*. I do." She tossed her hair over her shoulder and turned her back on him. "I really do."

Hamish had never taken well to being beaten at a game by his sister, and he wasn't about to start letting a woman beat him now.

Leaping up, he rushed for her, and wrapped his arms around her waist. He hoisted her into the air and spun around and around.

"Hey, get off me!" She squealed, tearing at his arms, which were locked around her, and kicking her legs. "Get off me."

He laughed and ran down the beach with her, toward the water.

She wriggled and writhed, swore and kicked. "You bastard. I'll kick your fucking ass for this!"

"I should wash your mouth out in the ocean for all your cursing," he said, striding into the first few inches of the waves.

"You wouldn't dare. You..." She was breathless and squirmy.

He stopped and curled himself over her, his chest to her slim back, clamping her to him as he bent forward. She was warm and soft in his arms and her hair smelled of a mixture of smoke and sweet larkspur. But she was also like a feral cat waiting to hiss and scratch at his face the moment he gave her room to.

He linked his fingers at her waist and set his mouth by her temple. "You don't think I'm brave enough to wash your mouth out?"

"I'll kill you. I swear, Hamish. I'll kill you for this. Let me go." She huffed. "Let me go."

He tightened his grip further. "What if..." he said onto the shell of her ear, her flesh soft on his lips. "What if I don't want to let you go?"

Her wriggling stopped. She was breathing hard. So was he. The sound of the curling waves rolling over themselves filled his ears and he wondered what he'd get next—Astrid the wildcat or the gentle woman who'd braided his hair and invited him to her bed?

"What do you mean?" she asked, her body stiff.

"What if I don't want to let go?" he whispered hoarsely. "What if I want to keep you here?"

"Here? On the beach?"

"No, here, in my arms."

"You fool, you don't know what you're saying."

Oh, but he did. Holding her, being so close to her… It was strangely like coming home. To a new home, perhaps, but a place he'd longed to be but hadn't known the way to.

"Hamish, stop being an idiot," she said, dragging at his sleeve.

"Why am I an idiot?"

"You don't know what you're saying." She huffed.

He straightened and spun her to face him, locking her once more in his arms.

A flash of wickedness crossed her eyes.

"Please don't knee me in the balls?" He braced for impact.

"Why shouldn't I?" She fisted his cloak, balling it tight as she glared up at him. "When you have me trapped, against you?"

"Which you hate so much?" He raised his eyebrows at her.

"Of course I do." She swiped her tongue over her lips. A few grains of sand clung to her right cheek. "I hate this. I hate you."

"You said you didn't hate me, earlier."

"'Haps I've changed my mind."

True. She did that a lot. "So shall we see how much you hate this?" Knowing her knee would likely ram into his balls at any moment, Hamish ducked his head and pressed his lips to hers.

She gasped and tensed and her grip on him tightened.

He pulled her closer, their chests pressing up hard and their legs connecting. Tilting his head, he deepened the kiss and used his tongue to probe for hers.

To his surprise, she opened up and let him in. Her tongue was warm and wet and she tasted so sweet.

He groaned with the sheer relief of giving into something he'd been burning to do.

"Hamish?" she said breathlessly. "What are you doing?"

"Do not worry about what anyone will say or angering your gods," he murmured. "Just let me enjoy having a beautiful woman in my arms for a few moments longer."

He cut off any reply with another kiss and as he explored the wet heat of her mouth, a rush of heat went to his groin. His cock stiffened and the urge to move up a level squeezed his very soul. If she asked him to lie with her now, he'd have no willpower to refuse. His fate would be sealed.

"Stop!" Suddenly, she pushed at him. "What the fuck?"

He was breathing hard, his blood running like fire through his veins.

"What are you doing?" she demanded.

"What I suddenly wanted to do."

"No." She waggled her finger at him. "You planned this. Following me to the bay. Spying on me swimming. Getting yourself trapped here in a storm. You're conniving and scheming, that's what you are, Hamish. You're sly and a liar."

"I am not!" He puffed up his chest and slammed his hands on his hips. "I am many things, but I am not a liar, and I refuse to apologize for following you here to be sure you were safe and ensuring that you had everything you needed."

"Oh, you're good." She mimicked his stance, hands on hips, feet spread wide. "Your wily god has given you the gift of honeyed talk, but I don't believe a word of it."

"If you don't believe words, believe actions." He frowned and stepped from the ebb of the waves. "If I were here just for *that*, don't you think I would have taken you up on your offer last night? I would have lain with you if that was all I wanted."

She shrugged nonchalantly. "You were just scared. Scared of me. Scared of sex."

"That's not true." His cock was still tingling. Clearly, it was still hopeful of a second invitation.

"Well, it was a one-time offer," she snapped.

His cock deflated.

"And you missed your chance." She pointed at the end of the beach, toward the large, otter-shaped rock. "And while the weather is good, you should go home, back to your village, your church, and your stupid holy book that tells you to do stupid things."

"I will go, but you should think about being more respectful to people who respect you and your beliefs, Astrid. It might make your life easier in the future, especially if you live in foreign lands." He turned. She was right he should go. And besides, he'd had enough of her blowing arctic-cold one minute and lava-hot the next. It was making him dizzy.

"What does it matter to you?" she shouted after him. "You won't be in my future. That is one thing I know as sure as the sun will set tonight."

He scowled and stomped his boots harder onto the ground as he walked away. It was time to draw a line under this stupid infatuation. Astrid was wild and feral and it was clear he wasn't going to be the one to tame her.

Chapter Seven

ASTRID TIDIED UP the bones from the hare and ate a handful of hazelnuts. She was glad Hamish had gone. He was a big, invasive presence when she wanted to be alone. And he was a pain in the ass too. Always spouting rubbish about life and gods and love.

She rolled her eyes and tutted. She'd send her prayers to Odin, Thor, and Freya so that she'd never have to see him again. Right this minute, he was walking back to Tillicoulty, past the copse where she'd seen amanita growing, the bend in the icy river, the place she'd spotted a goshawk roosting. Each step taking him and his annoying ways farther away.

Good.

She opened the sail a little to let the light into the cave and set about checking her arrows. She'd have to make some new heads; she was running low and hadn't finished making them at the meeting in the Great House. Haakon and Orm had annoyed her too much. She hadn't been able to stand breathing the same air as them and had had to get away. Far away.

And now she had an ocean to cross.

She began to whittle a piece of driftwood. Thanks to Hamish, she had plenty in the small cave next door.

As the arrowhead took shape, she thought of the kiss. That kiss. Hamish swooping his mouth down on hers as though knowing it wouldn't end well but not being able to stop himself. A little flush of heat traveled over her chest, tightening her nipples. His hold had been sure and strong and he'd tasted of ale and man and the ocean—a seductive combination for a woman who had gone a long time without sex.

Seductive. *What?* She huffed.

The boy was an innocent, or so he had her believe.

Was it true that he'd never been with a woman? It would have been easier not to believe him, but she did. He wasn't a liar—he was adamant about that—and also *why* lie about it? Most men would have been ashamed to go past their sixteenth summer without using their cock properly. It would be something to hide, not wear like a badge of honor.

She blew dust from the arrowhead. An image flashed into her brain—her sucking Hamish's cock. Hearing him cry out in ecstasy as he found out, for the first time, what it was like to know such bliss. It would be erotic, exciting, satisfying.

She'd ride his big body, hard, show him how to pleasure her, take what she wanted and let him do the same. His eyes would shine bright with wonder and he'd gasp her name, begging for more, for her to never stop.

Astrid wriggled on the rock she sat on, her heart rate quickening at the thought of what she'd missed out on. Perhaps she should have worked harder at persuading him the night before.

Maybe she shouldn't have been so quick to send him away.

When her quiver was full of sharp arrows, Astrid wandered out onto the beach again. She checked her fishing line and found a small fish. After unhooking it, she set it again. If she caught one a day, it would be something. But what she really needed was to go and set some traps.

So after eating the fish, finishing the last of the ale, and ensuring her fire was well stoked, she gathered her trapping equipment and wandered onto the forest track.

With her eyes and ears alert to prey and predators, she gathered herbs, nuts, and berries as she went. Pickings were slim, but there was more than there would have been at home.

Hamish's big footprints kept coming in and out of her line of sight. A solitary track of boot marks heading west. He wouldn't have been able to hide himself if he'd tried.

The goshawk swooped silently ahead, going from branch to branch. A good omen, she decided, that her traps would be successful here. So she stopped and set several, noticing rabbit droppings and a squirrel in the upper canopy that shook snow to the ground as it leapt.

In a clearing, she glanced at the imposing mountains. The white tips pierced the blue sky and she wondered what different things she might find in the foothills during summer months. Would there be edible berries she'd never tasted before? Tasty, little creatures to roast? Maybe even new flowers that could be used to dye linen. That had been one of her mother's favorite things to do, dye and weave. Astrid still had some of her rugs, back in her father's home.

She breathed deeply, the crisp air going right to the base of her lungs. Oh, she missed her father. Her departure had been sudden. There'd been no long goodbye. No chance to ensure he'd had everything he needed or to give Joseph a full set of instructions on every eventuality.

A thud started in her temple. A familiar sensation when she worried about her father's health.

Spotting a stream, no doubt one that ran to the big, icy river, she stopped and took a drink, scooping the chilly water into her palm and up to her mouth. It was then that she spotted a spawn of amanita again.

Perhaps that was just what she needed. An escape. A break from reality.

Before she knew what she was doing, she was gathering the tiny, red fungus from the mossy, fallen branch it was growing on. The scarlet domes, with tiny, white dots, soon filled her pouch. Quite the bounty—she'd have to be careful. An amanita ride could be pretty intense.

The sun went behind a cloud and when it came out again, Astrid noticed that the day's light was beginning to fade. But she didn't mind—it was still more than she would normally have had this time of year.

Soon, she was back at the cave. She'd caught another fish, which was good, and after heating water to wash, she gutted and ate it, wishing she had more ale. She was stuck with water now.

So she soaked a tiny piece of amanita in warm water, poking it about for a few minutes before drinking the water and discarding the fungus.

After that, she dragged a blanket around her shoulders and sat on a rock by the cave entrance to watch the sky fade to black.

It didn't take long for the familiar visions of amanita to arrive and she let out a sigh and leaned back on the wall.

The sky began to swirl. Great scoops of lilac and pink flushed with orange that drove east to west. Great birds were caught in the spiraling clouds, their batting wings distorting the rainbows around their tips. Odin's face appeared, blowing clouds from the perfect circle of his mouth. Then Thor with his shiny hammer knocking down on the cresting waves, destroying them and sending water in great, white arcs that teemed with silver fish.

It was good to see her gods at work.

The sunset colors became a great rug, the weaving intricate and the ends elaborate knots, and over it, her mother, the usual concentration line on her brow as she worked.

"Mother," Astrid murmured, her jaw heavy and her heart squeezing. "There you are."

She shivered. Her bones were getting cold. The colors were no longer vibrant, and her mother's face was fading into the indigo blue and night black of the sky. The sound of the ocean receded, and her eyes became heavy. Sleep was encroaching.

She didn't mind. In fact, she welcomed it. Sleep would be an escape from the pain of missing her parents, missing home, and her frustration with Haakon and Orm, who clearly didn't care that she was gone or for their gods anymore.

When she woke she stared upward, at the rough edges of the cave roof. Candlelight flickered over her and the scent of meat cooking in herbs hit her nose.

Her stomach rumbled. She couldn't remember crawling onto her furs the night before, but she must have. Which was unusual. On most occasions, she slept where she took amanita, her legs no good while the mushroom was still floating through her blood.

With a sigh, she wondered if dawn had arrived and with it a catch in one of her traps. Her traps. She hadn't checked them. She'd only just set them…so…so how come she could smell food cooking?

She sat and locked her arms behind herself, a rush of dizziness attacking her. "What the…?"

Through her blurry vision, she could see a big figure sitting by her fire stirring a pot.

She coughed, her mouth dry, and felt for her dagger. It was gone.

A rush of panic burst into her system and her heart rate shot up like an arrow.

"Ah," Hamish said, turning her way and then taking a mouthful of drink from a mug. "You're awake…at last."

"What in the name of all the gods…are you doing here?"

"Cooking, drinking ale. Waiting for you to tell me what the hell you were doing last night, sitting outside half-frozen, a wolf track not far from where you slept."

"I would have woken if a wolf had come." She likely wouldn't have, but Hamish didn't need to know that. Her heart squeezed. She'd been reckless and foolish. Lucky to get away with it.

"I doubt it. You were in the sleep of the dead." He gestured to the little pouch of amanita on one of the makeshift rock shelves. "That'll kill you, you know."

"Of course I know." She threw back a fur and a blanket and shuffled to the end of the bed area, gingerly touching her brow and wondering if a post-trip headache would attack her.

Luckily, it didn't. It was just her stomach and dry mouth to deal with.

"So why'd you take it?" he asked, pouring from a jug she didn't recognize.

"A bit of fun, in small doses. I like the colors."

He nodded slowly. "Strange way to have fun."

"You should try it sometime." She pushed her hair back from her face and sat on a rock next to him. "But now answer my question. What the hell are you doing here?"

He studied her, eyes narrowed. "I got halfway back to Tillicoulty and I came across a wanderer. He was heading toward the mountains, though whether or not he was going all the way, I don't know. You know what a wanderer is, right?"

"Of course I do."

"Just checking. Anyway, he had ale and candles, a few other things that he was selling, so I gave him a coin and told him where he could shelter, beyond the falls, downstream—there's a bothy there. He was glad of the local information."

"And?" She held her palms to the fire. Two grouse were roasting and a pan of broth boiling.

"And so I thought I'd bring what I'd bought back here. You haven't got much and it's weeks until spring will show herself."

"So can I have some ale?" It irritated her that Hamish had actually been so helpful. What he'd brought would be put to good use.

He poured her a mug. "It's flavored with yarrow."

"Let's hope it's not flavored with piss."

He passed her the drink then took another slug of his, looking at her from over the rim.

Several strands of his hair had sprung free of his braids and he had a smudge of mud on his brow. His dark cloak was on the rock next to him, and he'd shoved up the sleeves of his tunic. His forearms were pale and held a fuzz of hair and he wore a leather bracelet with beads around his right wrist.

"Tastes good," he said, then he stirred the pot.

"So you can go now." She pouted at him and clutched the mug so tightly, her fingers hurt. "You brought the stuff. Go now."

He let out a sigh.

"What?" she demanded.

"Can you not just drop it, for a few minutes?"

"Drop what?"

"The hostility. I'm not the enemy."

"Why should I drop it? You're not invited."

"That might be true. But I did bring you in from the cold and tucked you into bed. And I have brought supplies *and* I'm cooking you a meal."

"I didn't ask you to do any of that." Irritation had formed a knot in her belly.

"Astrid."

"What?" she asked.

"You're not fooling me, you know."

"What are you talking about?" A scowl twisted her face.

"I know what you're doing."

"I know what *you're* doing. You're being simple, that's what. No go back to your fellow simple villagers and get out of my hair."

"You're glad I'm here, so stop pretending otherwise."

"Why would I pretend otherwise?"

"To prove to me that you're capable, independent, tough. I know that already, Astrid." He sipped the broth from a long, metal spoon. "Mmm, it's good."

"Why would I waste time trying to prove anything to you? You, of all people."

"Because you like me."

"I do not." She huffed. "You're a Christian pain in the rear. I can't stand you. I wouldn't care if you fell off a cliff and the gulls ate your guts for breakfast."

He smiled, his cheeks balling and the flickering lights of the fire caressing his features. "How many men have you scared off with this *bitch from hell* routine?"

"More than I can count."

"Why?" He reached for one of the grouse and laid it on a flat rock. Then he set his sharpened seax on the plump, plucked breast and began to carve. "Why not let someone close?"

"Because I have a cold heart. Too cold to let anyone in."

"I don't believe you," he said quickly.

"Well, you should."

He sliced several cuts of meat then laid them on a flat stone and passed it to her.

She took them. "Why don't you believe me?"

"Because I see a warm heart in you, Astrid."

She pursed her lips as she poked at the grouse.

"I see you, the real you, and I know there's warmth in there."

"There isn't and—"

"And I'm intrigued, I'm curious, and I keep getting drawn back to you, whether I want to be or not. I tell myself it's to make sure you're safe, but there's something more." He frowned, as though his words were tumbling from him of their own accord. "And that more is... I don't know. I don't know what it is."

"So why not ask one of your stupid friends? Bryce or whatever his name is."

"You're right, Bryce is my friend, but he wouldn't understand. He'd tell me to stay well away from the icy-glared, sharp-tongued, bad-mannered, bad-tempered pagan who wishes us all dead."

"Smart friend."

Hamish chuckled and popped a slice of meat into his mouth. He watched her as he chewed.

It irked her that Hamish had thought about her so much, about her heart, about why he liked her. But at the same time…she also kind of liked it. "You should do as Bryce would advise." She shrugged.

"I know I should." He also shrugged.

They ate in silence. He passed her a bowl of steaming, thyme-laced broth and she took it without a word.

"It's dark outside?" she asked when she'd finished and her belly had a lovely, warm feeling.

"Aye, has been for some time. The moon is long up."

"But you can find your way back to the village in the dark." She hadn't said it as a question.

"Aye, I can."

"So…see you, then." She reached for her runestones and passed the small bag back and forth from one palm to the other. An action she always found comforting. "See you around… Or not."

"I'm not going anywhere." He shrugged.

"You have to. This is my cave. I'm telling you to leave."

"You seem so sure of that."

"About telling you to leave, *ja*."

"No, that it is your cave." He raised his eyebrows.

"My things." She pulled a face and gestured around. "Every-where."

"Things that you've put in *my* cave."

She frowned. "It's mine." Her lips pouted tightly.

"Astrid." He drained his ale and leaned back, arms folded. "I've been coming to this cave since I was a kid. I've slept in here before, sheltered from storms here before, cooked and played. It was my cave long before you ever stepped upon this beach."

She glanced around. It was true—there had been signs of a fire and a stash of wood when they'd found it.

"So I'm staying," he said. "At least until it's light—whether you want me to or not because really, this place is mine. Has been for years."

Her muscles tensed with irritation. "Fair enough, but try to kiss me again and I'll hack your toes off in your sleep."

"Maybe it's your unique charm that keeps me coming back." He laughed.

"Oh, piss off."

Chapter Eight

"**S**O WHAT'S THAT?" Hamish asked, nodding at the small, dark drawstring pouch Astrid was fidgeting with.

"Why do you want to know?"

"'Haps I don't, really." He rested his head back on the wall and closed his eyes. The meal had been satisfying and the cave was warm, if a bit smoky at times. And he had no intention of going anywhere.

"If you must know, it's my runestones," she said. "It's a way for the gods to speak to me."

He opened his eyes. "Really?"

"*Ja*, really. Has your god got runestones?"

"No." He nodded at them. "Will you show me?"

She hesitated, then, "I suppose."

Sweeping her hand over a section of ground to make a clear patch, she shook the bag then tipped three stones onto the floor. They rolled apart and landed a few inches from the fire.

Hamish peered forward. "How do you read them?"

"*You* can't," she said. "I have the gift and the knowledge. Many of my people ask me for readings."

"So what do they say?" He sat forward with his elbows on his knees and studied the little symbols on the top.

"It's a reading of the future, for me," she said. "They have not traveled far from where I sit."

"That's because you tipped them straight out, at your feet."

She frowned. "They have magical powers. If this reading had been

64

for you, they'd have landed near *your* feet."

"Ah, I see." His mouth twisted, unsure whether to believe any of it.

"This one..." She pointed at the one closest to her. It had a lightning bolt shape etched into the shiny surface. "Is Sowilō, the sun."

"Is that a good stone?"

Astrid was quiet for a moment. "*Ja*, though it's not one I draw often."

"Why?"

"It means self-awareness and self-knowledge and it encourages healing." She paused. "Though I am not hurt, so that can't be right. You would expect to find it after a war or a difficult journey."

Hamish looked at her small fingers turning the polished stone over and over. "Maybe it is not meaning physical hurt."

"You don't understand the runes." She frowned.

"I would agree, totally, but you told me you miss your father, and your mother. That is hurt, is it not?"

She pulled in a deep breath, her breasts rising and falling beneath her tunic.

He pulled his attention from them before she saw him looking at her chest. "And you feel your brothers have turned their back on the gods. They have disappointed you, an emotion that can feel like hurt."

"It's physical hurt," she said, looking away and letting her hair fall forward. "That is what it means."

"I get it." What he understood was that Astrid was in no rush to admit any kind of vulnerability to herself or to him.

Likely, she never would be.

Though when he'd found her in a deep sleep in the cold, and lifted her into her makeshift bed the night before, she'd been like a bairn in his arms. Small and soft and peaceful. He'd have enjoyed the moment more if he hadn't been angry with her for putting herself at risk the way she had.

She tucked the stone away and reached for another with a slanted H on the top. "This is Hagalz. Hail. This is not good."

"Why not?" He spotted a flash of unease in her eyes. "What does that mean? What is Hagalz?"

"It signifies destructive forces on the horizon."

"Destructive, as in…?"

"It could be nature, a big storm or the snow crashing down a mountain, a lake melting when riders are charging across it."

"Or?"

"It could be an encroaching army, a battle being planned and plotted, an enemy getting ready to enact his wrath."

Hamish didn't like the sound of that. "You think someone is going to attack us here? In the cave?"

"I cannot say for sure if it is here, or if it is your village. Your energy may have disrupted the magic. This is a call for action to take control of something that is out of control."

Hamish automatically glanced at his weapon and then at the entrance to the cave. He imagined King Athol with his men gathering outside ready to burst in and demand taxes, demand they take them to Tillicoulty. Demand Haakon renounced the crown he'd taken without asking.

"But this…" Astrid lifted the final stone. There was apprehension in her voice. And was there a slight shake in her hand?

"This is the mighty Perthro. I have only landed it twice before in moments of great need."

"And what is this rare rune telling you?" Hamish drew his thoughts away from battle and back into the quiet cave.

"Perthro is associated with a mystical bird that consumes itself in the fire then rises from its own ashes. It means powerful forces are at work for change. There may well be surprises, gains or rewards that I cannot imagine."

Hamish pressed his lips together as emotions danced on Astrid's face the way the shadows swayed on the cave wall. It was clear this stone had pulled her thoughts in different directions.

Which wouldn't be a bad thing. Maybe she'd stop telling him she hated him and wanted him to leave.

"So change is coming for you?" he asked.

"Change has already come for me. I'm here, aren't I?"

"That is true, but you don't want to stay in this cave forever."

"No. I don't. But I do not like surprises."

"But gains and rewards you do want. A pile of treasure, that's what you would like."

"It's something I need, for the afterlife."

"Do your gods not have enough of everything waiting for you?"

"Of course, but I do not want them to think I am poor when I go to Valhalla."

"Right now, you have very little material wealth."

"Ah, that is where you are wrong. Outside of Drangar, I have a treasure hole. It is full of many things, some from raids, some from trading."

"That's good, then." Hamish couldn't imagine worrying about taking things to heaven. He had enough to concern him already.

Suddenly, she swept up the stones and put them back in the bag. She set the bag beside a candle.

"Do you want an amanita infusion?" she asked suddenly.

"What? No."

"Go on. What else is there to do on a dark, cold night? It's hours before the sun comes up." She tipped her head and narrowed her eyes. "Unless you have other ideas."

Hamish felt his heart quicken. She'd flipped again. Now she was looking at him as though she liked him. Wanted him, perhaps. Being with her was like riding a skittish horse through the forest. He never knew which way he was going to be jolted.

"I need sleep," he said, nodding at the bed area. "My bones are weary."

"So sleep." She shrugged and looked away. The hard jut of her jaw returned.

"Do you want me to try the amanita?"

"Up to you." She shrugged.

"What does it do?"

A wicked grin spread on her face and she leaned forward, closer to him. "It gives you fantastical images to look at. It makes you feel out of your body, but at the same time, like everything in your body is more intense. And when you think about your worries, your problems, it's as if they don't exist, as if nothing matters."

"Is that why you didn't care about freezing to death last night, or being eaten by wolves?"

"That wouldn't have happened." She narrowed her eyes at him.

Hamish wasn't so sure, but he didn't push it. Perhaps Astrid hadn't been scared by either of those fates.

"I'll have a wee bit," he said. "Not as much as you took."

"You will?" She rubbed her hands together. "Great."

In an instant, she was breaking off a bit of red cap and poking it into hot water. She stirred it with great concentration then looked up at him with sparkling eyes. "I think you'll like it."

"Don't put me out in the cold, will you?" He wouldn't put it past her.

"There's not enough here for you to not know what you're doing. Just enough to get a...taste of it." She handed him the mug.

He sipped it, the musty, warm flavor spreading on his tongue. "How long does it take?"

She shrugged and sat back, crossing her legs and hooking her linked hands over her knee. "Depends."

"On what?"

"How susceptible you are to it."

He finished the small drink and wiped his hand over his mouth.

"'Haps your god will come to you," she said. "Tell me if he does. Tell me whatever you see or hear."

"To be honest, I'm just tired." He yawned. It had been a long day and he'd slept upright the night before.

"So lie down." She nodded at the bed area. "I'll watch over you, keep the fire stoked. You have fun watching the colors."

"I don't know if I'll see any." From a couple of mouthfuls of water that didn't even hold the amanita anymore? He didn't think so.

He shucked off his boots, his toes were tingling, and crawled onto the furs. His limbs were suddenly heavy. It must have been the mention of sleep.

He flopped down, hands above his head, and was glad of the warm cave haven they'd created. The bed was so much softer than he'd thought it would be. As if it had been made on a bed of moss, and the cave walls here were a vibrant shade of red that seemed to bleed from the darkest corners.

He let out a long sigh that weirdly seemed to take the air right from the tips of his toes and the ends of his fingers.

"How are you feeling?"

Astrid's face appeared before him, her hair hanging forward like flames dripping downward. The brightest orange and curling in bouncing spirals.

"I'm tired. That's all it has done." He yawned loudly and wriggled his tingling fingers and toes.

She giggled, the sound springing off the cave wall and traveling through his ears, down his throat, then settling in his chest like a vibration.

"I love that sound."

"What?"

"Your laugh."

She did it again and he let a broad smile spread on his face. It got so wide, his cheeks hurt.

"What can you see?" she asked, her eyes so blue now, it was as if he were looking at a summer sky.

"I see you."

"What else?"

"You are beautiful." He reached out and touched her hair, curling one ringlet around his finger. "So beautiful. And your hair is so soft." It was like silk, or the softest butterfly wing, the most delicate petal.

"My hair is soft, but you must tell me, Hamish, when the amanita makes your cock hard."

"What?"

"It will make your cock hard. It is why the people of Drangar like it so much."

He closed his eyes and concentrated on his groin. Was his cock hard? No.

"Do you promise to tell me?" she asked, her face so close to his now, he could feel her warm breath on his cheek.

"Aye," he said, tucking the lock of hair behind her ear. It was an effort; his arm felt heavy. "I'll tell you."

He felt like he was spinning. The gold of her hair and the red of the cave were all mixing together.

And then, suddenly, her lips were on his. Kissing him, her tongue probing in.

He let out a moan of approval and opened up for her. Was he dreaming or was this real? It certainly felt real, so he kissed her back and for once didn't fight the surge of arousal that gripped his belly.

"Hamish," she murmured. "Do you remember what I look like naked?"

"Aye, of course."

"Picture me now, on the beach. No clothes, my nipples hard as stones and my ass chilled by the wind."

"You were...perfect," he said. "So...perfect."

"I still am."

He smiled lazily, and as she kissed him again, he pictured her undressing on the beach—her beautiful, lithe, pale body being slowly revealed as she removed each item of clothing.

He groaned and shifted his hips. A rush of blood had gone to his cock and it was swelling inside his pants. Her image was so real in his mind and it was making him hot. Sweat tickled his underarms and his balls ached as his erection grew.

"Hamish," she whispered against his lips. "Tell me what you see?"

"You on the beach," he said, not opening his eyes. "Your breasts... Your ass... The soft patch of hair on your cunny." Her face had multiplied. There were three of her all blended into one and swaying softly.

"And what do you want next?" she asked, her voice sounding like it could be underwater. Distant and dreamy. "What do you want to happen?"

"I want you. To touch you." Was he slurring?

A sudden, firm pressure over his groin had him drawing up his left knee and groaning from somewhere deep in his chest.

"Shh," she said, kissing up to his brow and then smoothing his hair. "I can help you with this. It must be uncomfortable in your pants."

"Aye." He kind of nodded. "It is."

Her hands were moving over him now, caressing his cock through his pants. It hardened further and suddenly, he wished his pants were gone.

And then cooler air washed over his belly and his belt tugged as it was undone and then removed.

"Let me," she said in a hushed voice. "Relax and let me do this for you."

He dropped his forearm over his eyes and bit on his bottom lip as she tugged his pants down to his thighs. There was no part of him that wanted to stop her. He wanted her to give him some relief. Touch his cock and give him the pleasure.

"Hamish," she said, her voice musical to his ears now. "You have a fine, big cock."

He half-smiled. "Aye. I have."

"And it's so hard."

"Oh, help me, God." His entire body jerked and he fisted the furs beneath him.

She'd wrapped her hand around his length and as she'd squeezed, she'd rubbed it root to tip.

"Astrid." He uncovered his eyes and stared at her. She was knelt at his side, studying his cock as she gently massaged it, swiping her thumb over his slit each time she reached the top. "What are you...?"

"What am I doing?" She smiled at him, the gold wolf's-head brooch she wore flashed like lightning and left streaks in his vision. "I'm giving you pleasure, Christian boy. Something that is long overdue."

Chapter Nine

A STRID WAS HAVING fun. Lots of fun.

Hamish was like a sacrificial virgin sprawled out on the furs. For a big guy, the amanita had hit him fast, though he didn't seem too out of it—just pliant and lazy and open to suggestion.

Very open.

She smoothed up his velvety cock again, slowly, so slowly, knowing how heightened his senses would be. His skin would feel like every touch were a thousand touches, and his arousal would be all he could think of. It would fill his brain.

Oh, and he was beautifully aroused. His cock was pleasingly big for a Lothlender and had two perfectly straight veins running up its outer length.

He moaned again and she sought his balls, cupping them gently and rolling them in her palm.

His head tilted to the right and his jaw hung open as he squeezed his eyes closed. His cross pendant sat at an angle beside his throat.

She hoped he'd remember this moment if nothing else; he seemed to be enjoying it immensely.

Working him with precision, and in no rush, she massaged his cock until the muscles in his abdomen tensed to bricks and his breaths had picked up pace. He pressed the crown of his head into the furs, the tendons in his neck stretching.

"Come when you need to," she said. "Come like this, Hamish."

He didn't reply. He'd gone in on himself, a feeling she knew well and enjoyed.

Leaning forward, she kissed his stubbled cheek, his warm brow, and then his lips, enjoying the taste of his skin. He didn't kiss her back. His concentration was on what her hands were doing—playing with him, working his cock even harder.

And it was like rock. She was sure he was near.

She sat straight again and tightened her grip, giving a little twist to each up-and-down movement.

"Oh, God," he moaned as he flailed his arms out to the sides, palms up. "I need... I want..."

"I know what you need and want." She ran her thumb through his slit. It widened a fraction and a drip of pre-cum appeared. "*Ja*, that's it, like that." Excitement tripped through her. Soon, she'd see her virgin boy come and it was going to be spectacular.

Her pussy clenched and a fizz of anticipation gripped her belly. Her arm ached, but she didn't care.

He moaned long and low, completely uninhibited, and the sound sparked her own need for an orgasm.

But it was too late to ride him now—he was on the brink. She'd have to save that for another time.

"Come," she said. "Give in to it." She toyed with his balls a little firmer. They'd retracted, packed tight, and that told her everything she needed to know. "Hamish. *Ja*. Come."

He pulled in a breath through gritted teeth. A loud hiss. Then he expelled it in a long, deep wail.

His cock pulsed in her fist and the first rope of cum shot onto his belly. A few drips coated her thumb and index finger and she used that to lubricate her fast pace on his cock.

"Urgh!" He cried out, bucking beneath her. Hostage to pleasure. Bound to her. "Hell, that's good."

"*Ja. Ja.*" Her cheeks were flushed and hot and she was breathing fast. More release came as his cock throbbed and his entire body jerked. The moment of seeing him lost to ecstasy was almost enough to create a small shockwave of pleasure in her pussy. A tiny orgasm. Almost.

"Astrid...oh...fuck..." He gasped.

He pressed the heels of his hands to his eyes as he panted and the last spasms of his climax rippled through his body.

She slowed, then stilled, until she held his cock tenderly.

Would his orgasm have snapped him from his amanita haze or would it have sent him deeper? To a place where dreams and fantasy ruled before blackness descended.

Astrid sat for several minutes like this, watching Hamish's breathing return to normal.

When it did, it slowed to a point where she was sure he was sleeping. He'd gone deeper, into a slumber that looked black to her but would be vivid with color to him.

Carefully, she pulled up his pants, re-buckled his belt, then straightened the fur beneath his head. She covered him up to his neck, tucking him in warmly.

He'd be out of it for an hour at least, perhaps longer.

And when he woke? Well, that would be interesting.

HAMISH GROANED AND turned over. Softness followed him, as did the sooty scent of the fire.

Opening his eyes, he stared at the rocky wall and for a moment wondered where on God's Earth he was.

And then he remembered. Clam Bay. Cave.

He stretched his legs out—they were stiff. He'd obviously been asleep for a long time. Then he arched his back and yawned.

Finally, he sat and rubbed his eyes.

A pain in his head made him wince and he licked his dry lips, again wondering how long he'd slept.

Astrid.

Of course. It came back to him. Why he was in the cave. It was because of Astrid. That was why he was there. He was keeping a watch on the little wildcat who drew him to her with some strange kind of magic.

She was sitting on a rock beside the glowing embers of the fire. On her left thigh were several small stones and she appeared to be polishing one of them.

Her runestones.

She looked up at him. "You're awake. Finally." She tutted as though impatient with waiting for him.

He frowned. What the heck had happened?

"Thought you were dead," she added.

He glanced around. His vision was slightly off, as though his eyes were struggling to focus. When had he gone to bed? Had he drunk so much of the wanderer's ale that he'd passed out? Had the yarrow been some kind of weird drug?

The wanderer. Aye, that was it. He'd come back to the cave with supplies. They'd eaten grouse, drunk, and...

He looked at the runestones. Astrid had come up with some prophesies for the future using her little stones. And then...

He looked around as peculiar memories began to form.

Astrid's face floating above him, her hair like flames and her eyes the greenest green. Pleasure. The rock wall with vibrant, red swirls that danced and spun and wound around him. His entire body spinning, as if he were floating in the air and the wind was tossing him about.

"What... What happened?" he asked.

"Don't you remember?" She raised her eyebrows at him and breathed on one of the stones before rubbing it vigorously.

"I..." What was the answer to that? He couldn't remember what he couldn't remember. "I'm not sure."

He slid to the end of the flat rock and let his legs dangle over the end. A mug of ale sat to his right and he reached for it, sniffing.

"The ale is good," she said. "Drink."

He was too thirsty to wonder about it any longer and took a deep slug.

"The stones," he said. "The runestones. What did they do?"

"The runestones did nothing." She paused. "Unless, that is, you think they did."

He shook his head then pressed his hand to his brow. "No...I..." He glanced at the cave's entrance. The first licks of dawn were seeping through the sail. At least he presumed it was dawn. "Did you sleep?"

"*Ja*, for a while." She shrugged.

"But I...?"

"Slept for ages. You fell asleep fast. Straight after..."

"After what?" He looked around the cave, searching for clues. His boots were set neatly by the sack. The pile of firewood had been replenished. And on a shelf was a small scattering of drying red mushrooms.

Amanita.

Sipping the infusion. The taste. The spinning in his head. It all came rushing back to him. "I had too much of that." He pointed at it. "Why did you make it so strong?"

She tipped her head back and laughed. "Oh, you are so light. I hardly put any in it and you were..."

"I was what?" He glanced down at himself. His belt buckle was done up looser than he usually wore it.

Why?

"You really don't remember?"

He took another slug of ale to bide time. *Work, brain, work.* What had happened? He closed his eyes again, summoning memories.

All he got was a rainbow of colors dripping into each other.

Though as they merged Astrid's face again, over him, her lips on his, her eyes glinting, her voice sensual and calm.

His cock stirred and he shifted his weight.

"Surely, you remember," she said. There was a rattle as she tipped her stones back into their pouch.

"I remember." He kept his eyes closed. It was all tumbling back now.

His cock in her hand and her seductive words of encouragement. Her scent. Her taste. Her breath on his cheek and his neck. His balls tight. Her firm strokes and exploring fingers.

"Fuck," he muttered as he recalled ejaculating. His seed spilling from him as she'd massaged his cock until he could hold it off no longer.

He opened his eyes.

She was grinning at him—a self-satisfied grin that told him she very much thought she'd won whatever game she was playing.

"Why did you...?"

"Jerk you off?"

"Er... Aye."

"Why not?" She shrugged.

"But I was...out of it."

"You seemed to be having a pretty good time to me. And you didn't try to stop me."

"Could I have? After the amanita?"

She stood and walked to him, standing right in front of him and putting her hands on his shoulders. She lowered her face so it was close to his. "Hamish. You wanted me to touch your cock. You wanted me to make you come. You were begging for it, you would have done more, you would have fucked me, but I stopped you. I didn't want to take advantage of you in your inebriated state."

He stared into her eyes. She was a wily woman. Complex. Sly. A temptress. He should have been angry with her, but he wasn't. What she'd done had felt amazing, he remembered that much. He just wished he could have done it sober.

"You're a bad girl," he said, cupping her chin, his fingers pressing into her cheeks. "But I like it."

"Ha, you *think* you do."

"No. I do. I really do." He stared into her eyes, searching and examining. She fascinated him utterly. What went on in her head? She'd given him pleasure, yet she seemed to be the one basking in pleasure now. "You don't scare me, Astrid. Remember that. I'm not frightened by you."

"You should be, Christian boy."

"I'm not." Unblinking, he stared deep into her eyes.

Suddenly, she stepped away, toward the sail. She flicked it open. The day was more progressed than he'd expected and light flooded in.

"Where are you going?" he asked, supping more ale. It was cool and delicious on his dry throat.

"For my morning swim. Want to join me?"

Before he could answer, she disappeared.

He jumped to his feet. A wave of giddiness crashed over him and he flattened his palm on the cool wall for support. He waited for it to pass.

From now on, he'd treat amanita with the greatest respect. And by that, he meant he'd give it a wide berth.

"Damn it," he muttered, stepping past his boots. "Looks like I have to brave the cold sea to prove myself."

He followed her out. The sky was scattered with clouds, but the sun was shining, at least for now. The oystercatchers were busy to his right and the sea had washed up several more planks of wood from the Vikings' boat. They were twisted with rope and weed and there appeared to be a broken barrel amongst it.

Astrid was striding toward the spot she'd swum a few days before.

He followed her, and an image of her holding his cock, the lazy, hazy way she'd worked him, drifted back into his memory. A rush of blood to his groin went with it.

A cold dunk in the ocean might be exactly what he needed.

She stopped by the rock and tugged off her pants. When she removed her tunic, no breast strapping today, her ass was toward him.

All round and cute and the perfect handful.

He kept on walking. "Fuck it," he muttered, his cock swelling further. "What is it about her?"

She tossed her long, silken hair over her left shoulder then turned and looked at him over her right. Her breasts were pert and high, her nipples tight, and she pressed her hands to her waist and jutted out her chest.

In that moment, his breath caught.

There was surely no goddess as beautiful as her. Never in all of his life had he thought he'd see such a vision of perfection.

It was all he could do not to break into a run. Forget everything he'd ever promised God and his mother about waiting for marriage and beg her to lie with him. Spread her legs and let him sink deep. So he could rid himself of this aching hunger. Satisfy the need that gnawed at his soul.

"Come on!" she called, then she turned and ran into the cold waves with her arms in the air.

He broke into a run, tugging at his tunic as he went. His bare feet sank into the sand, crunching with each step. By the time he'd reached the rock, he was tearing at his belt and shoving at his pants.

She was waist-deep and turned to him, her face aglow with the cold. "This will shrivel your cock," she called with a cackle.

That could be a good thing, the way he was rushing to full hardness.

Her attention drifted to his erection. "May the gods be with you. That is going to be uncomfortable when it hits the water."

"Let me worry about that," he said, striding into the waves the way she had done. Without hesitation or delay. But dear Lord, it was icy. He was sure it was freezing the hairs on his legs as he went into the water up to his knees, then deeper.

She was watching him, shivering as she did so.

He stubbed his toe on a rock, ignored it, and then struck forward, submerging himself, head included, and let the thousand sharp daggers of cold pierce his skin, and his cock.

When he surfaced he was right next to her and he shook his head, spraying her in freezing droplets.

She squealed and stepped away. "Hamish! You bloody idiot."

But Hamish wasn't having any of it. If she was so insistent that he join her, she'd have to play his game now.

Chapter Ten

"**B**LOODY IDIOT, AM I?" Hamish shouted, reaching for her and hurling even more cold water into the air.

Astrid squealed again and pushed forward into a wave. It nipped her skin and pinched her nipples. When she swam a few strokes the chill went between her legs, seeping into her, cooling her from the inside out.

Suddenly, a hard arm wrapped around her and she was dragged back against a big chest.

"Hey!" She wriggled.

He let her go and she stumbled and went under the water. Her scalp screamed with the cold, seeming to shrink around her skull. But that didn't stop her and she swam as fast as she could, heading to the rock she'd swum to before.

The waves were gentle around her when she came up for air, gasping at the chill penetrating through her. She wouldn't survive long in water this cold, but it was as cleansing as it was invigorating.

"Astrid!" Hamish called.

She was aware of him coming up behind her.

Suddenly, a face appeared in front of her. It wasn't human. It had big, brown eyes, a perfectly round, shiny, black snout, and magnificent, white whiskers.

"Oh!" She stopped abruptly and her feet hit the rocky floor.

Hamish was beside her. "You've seen a seal before, right?"

"*Ja*, of course. Just wasn't expecting it."

The seal blinked, looked from her to Hamish, then was gone in a simple, arcing glide.

"Would have made a good meal," Hamish said, air puffing out in front of him.

"Shame you were too slow."

He laughed. "You were closer to it."

"And without my dagger."

She didn't wait for him to reply. It was time to get out before her toes fell off as icicles and her nose went permanently blue.

Within a minute, she was striding from the waves, the air seemingly just as cold on her wet flesh as the water had been. Like Hamish, her breath hung around her and she grabbed her clothes.

"No, don't waste time dressing here," he said, linking his fingers with hers. "Get up to the fire. Warm your skin."

He marched forward, his own clothes clasped in his free hand.

She followed at a fast pace, almost running to keep up with his speed. Her breasts jiggled and she studied the slope of his shoulder, where it connected to his neck. It was thick and wide and there was a raised, red scar across it.

"How do you get that?" Her teeth were starting to chatter and her jaw ached.

"What?" He walked quickly.

"The scar...on your..." She reached out and touched it.

"I fought a wolf."

"What?" Really? Had he?

He laughed, though it was cut short by a full-body shiver. "A few summers ago. It sneaked up on me while I was getting a kill from my trap."

"Asshole wolf."

"Indeed."

"Did it live?"

"What do you think?"

She was going to retort that she didn't think he had it in him to kill a wolf. But right now, looking at his tall, strong, lean body that was roped with muscles dancing beneath his flesh as he walked, he looked very capable of killing a wolf with his bare hands.

They reached the cave and he shoved back the sail, almost pushed her in, then was immediately at the bed area.

Astrid stood, frozen, and stared at the fire. It felt as if the cold water had gotten into her brain.

"Here," he said, throwing a thick fur over her shoulders. "And sit." He all but rammed her onto a rock. "I'll get the fire going."

He didn't bother to throw a fur around his own shoulders and instead squatted naked by the dying fire and began to stack a tepee of wood and kindling so it could catch again from the embers.

She shivered and pulled the fur tighter. His cock was flaccid but still long and she saw now that he had a triangle of darker hair at his sternum that spread out to his nipples.

"I'll soon have us warmed up," he said. "Though it was a dumb idea to swim in a winter sea."

"Who is the dumbest? The one who wants to do it, or the one who does as he's told?" Her lips were so cold, they barely moved.

He chuckled. "'Haps you have a point."

Why didn't Hamish seem to have any problem talking? She stared at the flames bursting upward and felt the first lick of warmth on her cheek. Cold-water swimming was always exhilarating and afterward, she enjoyed the sense of being reborn into the day. Almost like a new start, a fresh layer of skin, cleansed air in her lungs.

Hamish set the bowl of broth over the fire, on a stick, to warm. It was only then that he stood, tall and broad, and reached for a blanket to throw around his shoulders.

"You do that every day?" he asked.

"Ja."

"Is it just you or the way of your people?"

"It is the way of our people. It keeps us strong, reminds us that we are alive."

"It does that, aye." He cupped his hands together and blew into them.

"Though we like to bathe too, more than your people."

"'Bathe'?"

"*Ja*, a barrel of hot water, before the fire. Soap made with rosemary, or lavender or thyme." She closed her eyes. Thinking of the soap and its gentle, clean smell reminded her of her mother. "It's something I really loved to do."

"So you miss it?"

"I do."

"Then I'll get a barrel and make you a tub of hot water to bathe in." He paused. "And there's rosemary just beyond the rock. I'll scent the water with that. And I'll keep adding more hot water when it cools and you can stay there until your skin prunes."

She studied him. "Why? Why would you do that, Hamish?"

"Because you said you missed it." He smiled, just a little, the right side of his mouth tipping upward. "And I saw a wee warmth in your eyes when you spoke of it."

Her heart squeezed. It was annoying that it did because Hamish was irritating. Yet here he was saying he'd do something nice for her and making her like him.

"Right now, I'm cold. There was no warmth in my eyes."

He shrugged, like he didn't believe her, then moved to sit next to her on the rock.

"What are you doing?" she asked, looking at the fire again. It was beginning to roar, the smoke thankfully heading to the opening at the cave entrance.

"Sharing body heat. Your lips are still blue."

When he wrapped his arm and half of his blanket around her, Astrid didn't complain.

"Your hair is a mess again," she said, looking at the braids that were a tangle of curls.

"I guess my hair prefers to be wild and free." He chuckled.

She reached up and pulled one of the leather bands from it. Then another and another. Curl after curl sprang loose, a few drips sitting on the ends.

"I appreciate you trying to smarten me up," he said, his face close to hers.

There was something so pure and good in his eyes that a rare pang of conscience dug at her. "I'm sorry, Hamish."

"For what?" He frowned.

"For... For you know?"

"Nope." He shook his head. "I don't."

"For... For encouraging you to take amanita when you weren't used to it."

"Ah, that." He nodded slowly and reached up with the blanket pinched between his fingers. He soaked up a few drips from her hair that were hanging by her cheek. It was a gentle, caring gesture.

"It was... I mean, I didn't give you much and I wouldn't have left you on your own for the wolves to feast on, but I..."

"But you shouldn't have taken advantage of me?" Still, he looked intently at her, as if knowing what was on her mind and just waiting for her to say it.

She frowned. "You didn't complain."

"I was not myself."

"No, but..." She bit on her bottom lip. "You did seem to enjoy it."

"Did you?"

"Did I what?"

"Did you enjoy it? Did you enjoy touching my cock?"

A drip was running from his temple on a track to the angle of his jaw. She caught it on her fingertip. Suddenly, she was aware of her heartbeat. It thudded in her chest and her pulse rang in her ears.

"Astrid?" he whispered. He was so close now, if she tipped forward a few inches, she could kiss him.

"*Ja.*" She nodded. "I did enjoy it."

A sudden, heated intensity seared over his eyes and his nostrils flared as he breathed deeply. "But why did you?"

"Why did I?"

"Why did you touch me…make me come like that?"

"Because I wanted to. Do I need another reason?"

"I suppose not, but what bit of it did you want?" He paused. "To see my cock, feel my hardness, see my cum?"

She shook her head. "No, I wanted to watch your face as you found pleasure. Watch you give into it, lose control just for a few seconds as ecstasy claimed you."

"Fuck," he muttered. He slid his hand into her wet hair, cupping the side of her head. "And did you? See all of that?"

She swallowed, her throat dry, thoughts of being cold leaving her. She was heating up, her breasts were tingling, and her pussy quivered. "I saw all of that. You didn't disappoint."

"Is that a compliment?"

"I'm just saying." She shrugged one shoulder.

"And what if…?" he said, sliding his fingers to her nape and drawing her face even closer. "And what if I said I want to watch *your* face as you find pleasure? What would you say, Astrid? Would you let me?"

"I would, but you are forgetting?" The pleasure point between her legs pulsed, sending a tremble up to her belly and down her inner thighs.

"What am I forgetting?" His voice was low and deep, seeming to come from his chest.

"Your God. You promised to not lie with a woman until you are married."

"Will you marry me?" He raised his eyebrows.

"What! Fuck no. You bloody idiot. Are you—" Her eyes widened in shock. What a thing for him to say. As if?

His mouth was on hers, a heated, urgent kiss that had her reaching for him as he dragged her close. Their tongues tangled and he held her head just where he wanted her as he delved deeper.

She moaned and clung to his shoulders. She was hungry for it, hungry for him, but what was the point when he wouldn't take her? Wouldn't give her the satisfaction she was craving?

"Hamish," she gasped. "But…you… What about…?"

"That abstinence rule was all well and good until I met you," he said hoarsely as he shucked the blanket from his shoulders. "Until then, I could resist any woman. I could make my promise in church, to my mother, but now… Since the first day I saw you, it's been chipped away at, that promise, piece by piece, and now…"

"'Now'?" She ran her hands into his hair.

"Now it's gone. And I don't care. Fuck, I just want to lie with you, Astrid. May I?"

His handsome, earnest face was flushed as he waited for her answer. She had the feeling if she said *no*, he'd respect that, walk away. In fact, she knew he would. That was Hamish. But she didn't want to say *no*. She wanted this man. Her very own virgin to play with. She wanted to show him everything she knew and teach him exactly how to pleasure a woman.

"Lie with me." She gasped. "*Ja*, fuck me, yes, but just don't come until I tell you to."

"I'll try, but I can't promise." He flashed her a grin then was kissing her again.

The fire was roaring as he stood, taking her with him. Then she was in his arms for a moment before he was laying her on the soft furs. The cold water felt like a lifetime ago. Now she was warm and her skin alive as his big body rested over hers and he kissed across her cheek to her neck.

She wrapped one leg over the back of his thigh and ran her hands to his bare ass, cupping it and squeezing it, dragging her to him.

He moaned. His cock was hard again, prodding at her hip.

"Hamish," she murmured.

"Mmm…"

"You do know I'm not going to marry you, right?"

"Aye, I know." He slipped a little lower, kissing over the rise of her left breast as he cupped the right.

She closed her eyes and arched her back as he sucked gently on her nipples and fondled them to hard peaks.

"Mm, more," she murmured, smoothing her hands up to his shoulders.

He gave it, his teeth catching on one nipple and his fingers squeezing the other almost to the point of pain.

"Oh, *ja*, like that." She groaned. "Oh…fuck, *ja*."

Encouraged, he kept on, worshipping her breasts until she was squirming. It was like there was a connection between her nipples and pussy. Each flick and caress made her tight between her legs and stoked the need.

He lifted his head and stared at her face. "Am I doing it right?"

She nodded. "So far…but…"

"But what?" He frowned.

"Go lower?"

"'Lower'?"

"*Ja*, kiss me down there. Lick me down there."

He opened his mouth to speak then closed it again. He nodded, once, then set about trailing his mouth down her body.

Astrid adored a man's mouth on her pussy. It was such a powerful way to climax. But never had she had a virgin do it to her. She'd better not get her hopes up. How skilled could he be?

Chapter Eleven

HAMISH'S HANDS WERE everywhere as he moved down Astrid's body, as though wanting to touch her everywhere at once but not knowing where to begin.

Astrid closed her eyes and touched him where she could reach. She was damp down below and her breaths were quickening in anticipation.

He dipped his tongue into her navel as he slid his hands from her ankles to her thighs.

She parted her legs, allowing him to settle between them.

His kisses spread lower, to the patch of her hair at her pussy, and then he pulled back. Looked at her—looked at her intently—down there.

"Like what you see?" she asked, fingering through her pubic hair.

He nodded then swallowed noisily.

She swiped her fingers over her nub, brushing her soft folds, revealing herself. "This is where it feels really good for me."

Again, he nodded.

"Kiss me here, like you did my nipples."

"I can do that."

"I just bet you can."

His eyes fluttered shut as he leaned forward.

The next thing Astrid knew, she was canting her hips and dragging up her knees to clasp against his shoulders. "Oh!"

He'd taken her into his mouth, a gentle suck that was quickly followed by a few firm flicks of his tongue.

Her pussy clenched and her abdominal muscles tightened. "In the name of Freya, oh…yes…like that." Fuck, how did he know how to do it just right?

He upped the pace a little.

A groan caught in her throat and she ran her hands into his hair again, tugging it as she rolled her hips beneath him. It was so good. He was a damn natural. It was a crime no woman had experienced his tongue on their pussy until now.

"Do you like it?" he asked, kissing her inner thigh and rolling her nub under his fingertips.

"*Ja, ja*, can't you tell?" She pulled on his hair. "Don't stop."

"Just checking." He flashed her a sinful grin then stroked his tongue up through her folds.

She curled her toes and reached down to circle her nub. Fast. Hard. Intense. She stared at his rapt face.

He watched for a few more moments then set his fingers over hers and followed her movements. With his free hand, he slid two fingers into her slick pussy.

"Oh…oh…" She panted. "*Ja*. Like that. In deep."

He delved higher into her hot wetness and looked up at her. Something told her he was studying her face, the way she had his. Etching every expression onto his memory and greedy for each twitch and flicker.

"I want your cock," she gasped. "Now."

To her surprise, he didn't give it. Instead, he pushed her fingers aside and worked her nub again with his mouth as he pumped in and out of her. He was fucking her with his long fingers.

"Oh, *ja*…" she moaned, dropping her head back as all of her muscles stiffened. The pressure in her pussy was growing. "Oh…don't stop."

Astrid reckoned a rock fall could tumble down over them, from the mountains, and she wouldn't have noticed and he wouldn't have stopped.

He worked her relentlessly and she was lost to it. Lost to sensation and the soft, sweet sounds of him building her to orgasm. "I'm going to come." She gasped, locking her legs against his broad shoulders. "Oh...oh..."

It was there, a great expulsion of energy that had stored up in her pussy to become sheer bliss. For a honey-sweet moment, she held it in, held her breath too. But then it had to come out and she wailed long and low, springing forward as her nub throbbed within the suction of his mouth and her pussy clamped around his fingers.

She canted her hips, wanting more of everything he could give her as the white-hot fingers of ecstasy spread around her body. She was crying out, wailing, gasping for breath and she didn't hold back. She let him hear it all so that he'd know he'd gotten it just right.

"Oh...you...are...a natural." She gasped, tugging on his hair so that he'd lift his face and look at her. "So...fucking good...Hamish."

He rose up above her, his face over hers, his fingers still buried deep.

There was a self-satisfied flash in his eyes and his mouth and chin were slick with her arousal.

She stared up at him and cupped his rough cheek. She was struggling to catch her breath and her belly was juddering with the aftershocks of pleasure.

"You taste amazing," he said. "I never even thought...that you would like that or..."

"I like it a lot." She widened her legs. "Now fuck me. Fuck me, Hamish. Now."

He locked his arms on either side of her head and looked down at where his rigid, dark cock was angled at her spread pussy.

Astrid stilled with her hands wrapped around his thick biceps. She didn't want to break the spell for him. This was his first time. His first moment of entering a woman.

Fuck, it was hot.

"I want it so bad," he murmured. "I want you so bad."

"So have me." She shifted her hips, welcoming him.

He touched the shiny tip of his cock to her entrance then eased in just an inch.

"That's it," she encouraged. "Give me it all."

He curled his hips and entered her some more, watching the smooth length of his cock disappear. There was no rapid plunge, as she'd expected. No desperate ride to full depth. Instead, he was controlled and slow, as though savoring every inch of her.

Her pussy quivered around him, soft yet tight against his invasion, her orgasm lingering deliciously.

"Ah, fuck..." he said, his eyelashes fluttering. "You feel amazing."

Astrid didn't answer. His flushed cheeks and glistening eyes held her as captive to him as he evidently was to her.

"Oh, God..." He went deeper, deeper still until his cock was buried balls-deep.

She touched his face, drawing his gaze to hers. "Hamish."

A tense line etched over his brow. "I can't... Oh..." His jaw slackened and his mouth hung open.

She clenched around his thick girth. He was so solid and had filled her absolutely.

He grunted. "What are you...?"

"You like that?" She clenched again, then again.

His entire body lurched, then he screwed up his eyes and pulled almost out. He was quick to penetrate her again, fully, with one wild thrust of his hips. A feral cry left his mouth and he collapsed down on her.

Her virgin was no longer a virgin.

He rolled his body over hers, grinding against her as he gave two more near violent thrusts. His strangled moans blew hot by her ear and he shook in her arms.

Excitement winged through Astrid, but as it did, she realized she was struggling to breathe. His weight was on her entirely, his arms having collapsed.

She shoved at his shoulders and wriggled. "Hey."

He didn't move.

"Ha...Hamish." She whacked his shoulder. "Get off."

In a rush of slick flesh and a long groan, he was off her and at her side.

She dragged in air and pushed her hair from her cheeks.

Staring up at the cave roof, he was breathing hard, his hands on his chest. His cock was still hard and glossy with moisture.

"I'm sorry," he said.

"For what?" She stared up at the rocky imperfections above her. Her heart was still beating wildly.

"You said..." He dragged in air. "Not to come until you said, but..."

"But what?"

"It felt too damn good." He shifted to his side and reached for her hand, kissing her knuckles. "Your cunny, it felt so good. Hot and wet and tight and then you did...that thing... I..."

She giggled. "Don't worry. No man can resist me when I do that."

"I certainly couldn't. Not on my...you know, first time."

"Well, at least I believe you now, that you were a virgin."

"I told you, why would I lie?"

"Men lie."

"I don't." He reached out and circled her right nipple with the tip of his finger. "I don't see the point. Life is confusing enough."

"Ha, you're right there."

"What's confusing you?" he asked.

"You really want to know?"

"Aye, of course."

"You."

"Me?" He stilled his finger just below her nipple. "Why?"

"I thought you were a Lothlender with nothing to offer. A poor fighter, a Christian, good for nothing other than farming, but…"

"'But'?"

"But, maybe I like you a bit." There, she'd said it. No going back.

He chuckled and stroked over to her other nipple. She liked his gentle, searching touch.

"I'll take that," he said. "Because I can't imagine you like many people. I'm honored to be one, even if you only like me a bit."

"I like my father. I *love* my father."

"Anyone else?"

"Love?" she asked, raising her eyebrows. "No."

"Not even Haakon and Orm?"

"Not at the moment, no."

"So you love your father and you like me…a bit. And that's it. Am I right?"

"*Ja.*"

"Then I am a happy man." He lifted up and kissed her.

And she liked it a lot. His kisses were warm and soft and he was kissing *her*, not just some woman he wanted to fuck. She was his one and only and that knowledge sneaked into her heart.

"Wait a minute," she said, pushing at his shoulders. "I have to…"

"You have to what?" He moved aside as she sat. Quickly, she scooted to the edge of the bed and stood. A drip of moisture slid down her inner thigh.

She frowned and reached for a bowl of water, sloshed a cloth into it, then wiped herself clean thoroughly.

"What are you doing?" He was watching her.

"Wiping away your seed." She wrung out the cloth and did it again, the cold water a shock. "Next time, take your cock out before you come. We don't want little Astrid or Hamish running around when the leaves fall."

For a moment, he was quiet and then, "There'll be a next time?"

She looked up at him and laughed. "Hell *ja*, the nights are long and cold. What else have we got to do?"

He grinned. The grin turned into a laugh.

She laughed with him. "As long as you promise to last longer."

"That will come with practice." He patted the fur at his side. "Why don't we start practicing again now, eh?

Astrid grabbed the bottle of ale and threw a log on the fire. She moved the bubbling broth aside.

Her new lover was eager for more.

Was she complaining?

Hell no.

She let her gaze roam his body. From his cheeky, hopeful grin and flushed cheeks to his broad, hair-dotted chest, solid abs, still-erect cock, to his long legs and long feet and toes. His skin was pale, like hers, and a little red in places. A sheen of sweat sat in the hair at his sternum and on his brow.

He cocked his head and studied her as she moved toward him. The light of the flames lit his eyes. His pupils were wide and his lids heavy.

She drank deeply from the ale then passed it to him.

As he drank, she crawled back onto the furs to his side. Once there, she set her hand flat on his chest and pushed.

"Hey…" A dribble of ale landed on his chest hair.

She took the bottle from him and set it aside. "Lie down, Christian boy. I'm going to show you what it's like to get fucked rather than doing the fucking."

His head landed on a white fur, his bright hair fanning out on it in a riot of curls. "Do what you want with me." He grinned.

Astrid didn't think she'd ever known a man to smile so much. He was clearly having a great time.

"Remember, don't come inside me again. We're not a married

couple trying to make heirs."

"I won't."

She paused and gave him what she hoped was an *I-mean-it* look.

"Hey." He held up his hands. "I promise I'll tell you if I'm going to, and I'll…"

"Pull the hell out." She straddled his upper thighs, his cock nudging her belly.

"Aye, I'll pull the hell out." He reached up and cupped her breasts, covering them with his big hands.

She leaned forward and set a kiss on his lips. "You ready for me?"

"Aye, I'm ready for you, wildcat."

"'Wildcat'?"

He chuckled. "That's what I think of you as."

"Why?" She reached between their bodies and took hold of his solid cock.

He hissed in a breath as she squeezed gently.

"Why? Why do you think me a wildcat?"

"Because you're quick to hiss insults that cut to a person's soul."

"I'm glad you've noticed." She kissed him again and ran her fingertip over his slit.

"I'm sure I have a few scratches from your claws."

"Do you regret them?"

He ran his hands to her ass cheeks. "Scratch away, wildcat."

"So you…?" She swallowed and frowned.

"What?" He looked up at her.

"So you don't want me to stop…stop being…?"

"Stop being who you are?" He shook his head and matched her frown. "Hell no. Never change, Astrid. Please. Always be who you are right now."

She was quiet. No one had ever said that to her before. Everyone had always tried to get her to change—to be softer, kinder, more feminine. Unless she was on a battlefield or rowing a ship, then they wanted her to be stronger and uncomplaining and as skilled as a man.

But this man, this foreign man beneath her, with his strange god and strange ideas. He wasn't asking that of her. He wanted her to *never* change.

"You don't want me to change?" She double-checked her hearing was working.

"No." He smoothed his hands up her back and over her shoulders to cup her face. "I think you're smart and brave and beautiful and there is no one else like you on Earth." He swept his lips over hers. "Stay unique and incredible. It's what I adore about you."

Her eyes prickled, as though annoying tears might form. And crying wasn't her thing. So instead, she kissed him passionately, losing herself in the taste and feel of him as their tongues tangled.

His response was equal, his kisses full of desire, and his exploring hands hungry for her.

After a few moments, and any tears had dissipated, she lifted up and hovered over him, holding his thick cock at her entrance.

"Ah, fuck," he muttered, his eyes wide. "Astrid."

"Keep still," she said. "While I sit on you."

He bit on his bottom lip and nodded, clearly enrapt at the sight of her over him.

She smiled, warmth flooding her, then slowly took him into her body.

His fingertips tightened on her thighs, creating little dents and the tendons in his neck strained. "Ah... Ah... Aye, that's it."

The girth and length of him was impressive and she took it slowly, enjoying the denseness and the stretch.

"Oh, *ja*..." She tipped her head back and sat fully, her ass on his legs and her breasts jutting out.

"Fuck," he muttered reaching for her breasts again. "I never... I..."

"You thought people did it like animals?" she asked breathlessly. "A quick one from behind, a stallion and mare, a ram and ewe?"

"Well, no... I..."

She tipped forward, his cock shifting deliciously inside of her. "*Ja,* you did." She laughed softly and kissed the tip of his nose. "Which is good. You have so much to learn and I can teach you it all."

He ran his fingers into her hair, pushing it from her face. "What do you want me to do?"

"Nothing. I told you, I'm riding you. Just tell me when you're about—"

"To come...I know." He gritted his teeth, a tendon in his jaw flexing.

She rolled her hips, her ass cheeks clenching, and butted her nub up against his hard body. "Oh, that's it there." She set her hands on his chest, closed her eyes, and began to work herself to another spectacular orgasm.

Her visit to Lothlend had improved considerably.

And that was all because of one man.

Chapter Twelve

HAMISH TENSED ALL of his muscles and willed himself not to come. He had to hold it together. He had to prove he was a man, even if inexperienced. He wanted Astrid to think him a competent lover, if not a skilled one.

"Oh, *ja...*" She moaned and moved her hips in what seemed like a well-practiced rhythm. Rubbing the sweet, little spot he'd found in her folds against his body as his cock rode into her, onto her, within her.

He studied her face. Her eyes were closed and her long eyelashes were resting against her flushed cheeks. The slackness of her mouth told him her concentration was elsewhere.

He moved his hands from her thighs to her petite waist and pulled up his knees, the soles of his feet dragging at the furs.

Never in all of his life had he seen anything more beautiful, more erotic, more of a test to his self-control.

His first lover was beautiful and giving, and her sassy mouth and sharp mind made it all the more extraordinary that he was with her, like this.

He was a lucky man.

"Oh, Hamish... Fuck, I like your big cock," she said on a gasping breath. "Oh...*ja...*"

"You want me to stay like this?"

"I'm close again." She opened her eyes and stared into his. "Don't move and don't come."

"I won't." As he pinched her nipples and tugged gently, he hoped he could keep that promise.

"Oh, like that...more."

He was a little firmer with her nipples and it seemed to tip her over the edge.

She sped up, gyrating wildly on him, crushing their bodies together. A scarf-like flush went from her chest to her neck, a prickle of sensual heat. And then she wailed and clasped her hands over his, arching her back and tipping her face to the ceiling of the cave.

His cock throbbed. His balls were tight. The urge to come was intense. He was in a full-scale battle not to.

Her pussy squeezed and released his length. Moisture gushed from her.

She yelled out again, the sound going to his heart and his cock.

On and on, she rode him, as though eking out every drip of pleasure.

"Astrid," he gasped. "I... Fuck..." He gripped her waist. "I can't hold...off."

Suddenly, she was up, his cock having slipped from her. She grasped it tightly and rubbed with frantic energy.

"Oh, fuck." He propped onto his elbows and watched her hand on him. She moved so fast, it was almost a blur.

And his cum was there. He couldn't hold off another second. His breath trapped in his chest and his belly tensed. His balls constricted and he gave in to the need for release.

"Come," she ordered.

He was. The pleasure searing up his cock was hot and potent and dragged a roar from his chest.

She stayed with him, working him, her small, nimble hands seeming to touch all of his cock at once.

More pearly come basted his abdomen, then another and another shot. Had he ever come so hard and for so long?

"You did it," she said, her hair hanging forward in long, curly ropes. "You didn't come inside me."

He was breathing too fast to reply.

Suddenly, her tight grip on his cock felt almost overwhelming, as if he were overstimulated. He caught her wrist in one hand and wrapped his arm around her with the other.

He dragged her small, strong body over his so their chests were pressed together. "You look beautiful when you climax. You sound it too." He set his hands firmly over her ass, clasping her to him.

"I don't believe in not vocalizing pleasure."

"You've already taught me that." His throat was a little hoarse from his yell of ecstasy.

"You're a quick learner." She kissed him. It was different this time. The urgency had gone. It wasn't a prelude to sex—it was more indulgent, as though she liked kissing...liked kissing him.

Eventually, she pulled back and rolled off. She landed on her back at his side.

He missed her heat and slight body weight.

"We can't go back to the village now."

"You didn't want to, anyway," he said, then paused. "Why can't we?"

"Because...you know."

"What?"

"This." She flapped her hand between them. "Us."

"What's the matter with us?" He sat and reached for the ale, then took a drink.

"It's embarrassing."

A drip caught in his throat and he spluttered. "'Embarrassing'! Why?"

"Because..." She frowned and took the bottle. "You're you...aren't you?"

"Last time I looked." His heart had been slowing, but it picked up again.

"And it's…not right. This."

"Astrid." How had she gone from soft and pliant to hard and rigid so quickly? They were still naked, for God's sake. "I don't know what you're talking about."

"You're Christian, Hamish, and I've just given my brother seven shades of shit for marrying a Christian. Bloody hell, I've just stormed off, leaving him and Orm behind because of it."

"I did tell you I wasn't serious about asking you to marry me. I can't imagine you're the marrying type."

"I'm not."

"Good, neither am I." He'd always thought he had been, but maybe he'd have to adjust if it was Astrid he wanted to be with.

Was it?

"*Ja*, you are," she said. "You were saving yourself for marriage. So you obviously thought you would get married one day."

"I did. Until I met you."

She frowned at him and took another long drink. She passed the bottle back. "What do you mean, *until you met me?*"

He took her hand, not knowing if she'd snatch it back, despite the fact that only moments ago, she'd permitted him to touch her anywhere he pleased.

Her fingers were a little stiff, but she let him wrap his around them. He had a sudden urge to never let her go. Keep her hand in his.

But she'd never concede to that. Not in any number of lifetimes.

"I told you I don't want you to change, and if I asked you to become a Christian so we could marry, that would be changing you."

"Haakon did it for Kenna."

"You're not Haakon and I'm not Kenna. I have no desire for you to worship my god, only that we respect each other's gods and beliefs."

Her eyes narrowed and she studied him.

"You don't believe me?" he asked.

"I worry you are slick with your tongue, a serpent with the gift of words."

He laughed. "What? I told you, I don't lie. I'd only confuse my-self." He raised her hand to his lips, turned her wrist over, and kissed the delicate underside that was mapped with pale-blue veins.

"I don't need a husband."

"I'm not offering." He raised his eyebrows at her.

"So what *are* you offering?"

Hamish pulled in a breath. How he answered was important—he could tell by the set of her mouth and the tilt of her chin.

"Well?" she prodded.

"I'm offering," he said, "to keep you company while you wait out the winter here in this cave."

She was thoughtful for a moment. "And?"

"And I'll hunt, fish, set traps, and—"

"I don't need you to do that. I'm quite capable."

"I know you are, but I have to pull my weight if I'm eating too."

"That's true." She liked that he thought fairly.

"And I have local knowledge. I know the direction the wolves come from, where the best place is to catch pheasant and grouse."

She was quiet.

"Which you would figure out on your own, after a while, so you don't need me for that."

"No. I don't."

"But maybe..." He dropped her hand and scooted closer, pressed his palm to her soft cheek. "Maybe you could just use me for my body, to entertain yourself through the cold, dark nights."

"'Use you for your body'?" A glimmer of amusement spread in her eyes.

"Aye, I would be at your complete disposal. Do whatever you want with me."

"And what do you get out of it, Hamish?"

"Fine lessons in sex with the best and most beautiful tutor I could wish for."

"Like I said, you have a slick tongue." She raised her eyebrows, but there was an amused tilt to them. "You have a slick tongue, but let us eat and then you can get to work with it again."

"I can?"

"*Ja*. A man needs many hours to perfect the technique of going between a woman's legs with his mouth."

She untangled from the furs and stood, going to the fire.

He watched her graceful movements as she pulled on her clothes and knotted her hair on top of her head. Was she teasing him about many hours of using his mouth on her? Or was she being serious?

He shrugged and also stood. What did it matter? As long as they were getting down and dirty, sweaty and naked again soon, he was happy.

DAYS TURNED INTO weeks in the cave. Astrid was happy. An emotion she rarely felt.

Right now, she was curled up in Hamish's strong arms. Outside, the wind howled and the snow blew around as if it had no intention of landing anytime soon. The sea roared with each wave that crashed and a collapse of rocks to the east had spread mud and gravel almost down to the shoreline.

But inside the cave was warm. They'd improved the structure at the entrance and had a reasonable supply of food along with plenty of fuel. Which was just as well because the storm had raged for days with barely a break in between Thor's wrath.

She sighed and closed her eyes, snuggling closer into the curve of Hamish's neck. Breathing deeply, she filled her lungs with him. She adored his masculine scent. It was different to others. There was something more appealing about it, as though he were part of the ocean, the forest, the animals he knew so well.

Tiredness crept up again and she closed her eyes, welcoming it. They'd shared a small infusion of amanita several hours earlier then enjoyed blissful, surreal, orgasmic sex for what had felt like forever. She hadn't known where her body had ended and his had begun. A tangle of arms and legs, a slide of fingers, cock, and her wet pussy always ready for him. Eventually, as she'd swayed on her hands and knees, he'd taken her from behind, his cum landing on her ass cheeks before he'd flopped forward in exhausted satisfaction.

The inside of her eyelids glowed red, the color swirling and sparkling. The amanita was still playing with her.

As her body slumped into sleep, she let her thoughts merge with the colors, patterns drew themselves, images came and went.

And then one grew and stayed. It filled her vision and her heart.

Her mother. Beautiful, young, glossy-haired. She sat at her loom.

"Mother," Astrid said, her mouth heavy and thick.

Her mother looked up and smiled. This never happened in her dreams, even her amanita ones.

Astrid experienced a sense of longing in her heart she could hardly bear.

But then alongside her mother another figure came from the spiral of reds and oranges.

Freya. The goddess herself.

This was like no other vision she'd had before. It was an omen, a direct communication from her mother as she sat feasting with the gods.

"Astrid," her mother said, holding out her hand. She was still wearing the rings she'd died in. "My tempestuous, precious, only daughter. I see you. I see you now."

Astrid tried to nod, but her head was heavy.

"We see you," Freya added, her voice dreamy, her perfect lips smiling. "And we are here to tell you something."

What? Astrid wanted to scream. *What are you here to tell me?*

"It is about your future," her mother went on, her hair seeming to lift in a constant breeze. "Your future with a man—we have seen him. He has flame-red hair. He is not of your homeland."

Her heart squeezed. Were they talking of Hamish? The man keeping her warm during this isolated and cold winter?

"*Ja*, my child," Freya went on. "He is a good man, the only one who speaks to you with a true tongue, who sees you as you really are."

But he's Christian, Astrid wanted to shout. *He doesn't believe you exist, my much-revered goddess Freya.*

"And destiny holds many sons for him. Many sons with flame hair who will one day travel," her mother said.

"'*Travel*'?" Astrid managed to mouth.

"They will travel to claim their rightful kingdom. The Kingdom of Drangar in the north." Her mother's tone was sure and steady. "You will bear heirs for Hamish, strong, powerful heirs, three of them, who will finish your father's work, Astrid. They will unite Drangar and honor the gods with many sacrifices and festivals. It is only the sons of Hamish, son of Noah MacCallum of Tillicoulty, who can succeed in this mission."

Sons? Thoughts blustered through Astrid's mind. Images of three smiling, bright-haired boys appeared beside her mother. She affectionately touched their cheeks, their lips, their arched eyebrows.

Astrid thought her heart would squeeze itself so hard, it would stop beating. There was so much love inside of it. Love for her mother, for the sons she'd prophesized.

For Hamish?

Suddenly, the image that had been so real before her started to slide away and fade. Her mother's face became a shadow, the boys blended with her gown, and Freya slipped away.

Don't go, Astrid wanted to shout. *Please. Stay. Tell me more.*

The ache she felt at them leaving seemed to twist her soul. Her throat felt tight and her limbs wanted to run, to give chase, but they were heavy and wouldn't move.

"Astrid. Shhh, Astrid."

A voice came from above her, deep and soothing.

"I've got you."

Hamish.

She forced her eyes open. It was hard. What if they came back? What if she missed seeing her mother again?

Arms tightened around her and she was aware of a kiss pressing to the top of her head.

"Hamish?" she managed.

"You had a dream. It's the amanita," he whispered. "But it's over now."

"It was quite the dream." She curled her fingers into his chest hair.

"Tell me about it."

"I can't?" It was too precious. Too personal. It had opened her eyes to something she hadn't been able to see.

"Why not? Why can't you tell me?"

"I just can't." She pushed up from him, pausing when her head spun.

"Hey, it doesn't matter." He sat and tucked her hair behind her ear. "As long as you're well."

"Of course I am." She swung her feet to the floor, waited a minute, and then stood. "The fire needs attending."

"I'm sure it does." His voice was still lazy, sleepy. She was glad he hadn't pressed her to tell him about the dream.

But that was his way. If she didn't want to do something or say something, he just accepted it. And it wasn't because he was always agreeing with her. He just let her have her private thoughts and her own mind. She appreciated that.

A lot.

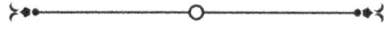

Chapter Thirteen

"**I**'M BORED," ASTRID said, peering out at the beach.

"So come back to bed." Hamish yawned.

"We've been in bed for days."

"I'm not complaining." He chuckled.

She stared out at the snowy beach. The wind scuffed over the surface, whisking up flakes from where they'd settled. The sea was busy crashing over itself and in the sky, amongst broken clouds, the sea eagle circled.

"We should go out," she said.

"What? No, it's cold. Why don't I warm you some water? You can bathe in the barrel again. You like that."

"And I have not long since done it." She threw him a glance. He was standing naked beside the fire and drinking from a mug.

Even though she knew his body intimately, seeing him like that, gloriously unself-conscious and strewn with muscle, made her pussy quiver. Would she ever stop wanting Hamish?

Perhaps not until she'd borne him three sons, as her mother and Freya had prophesied. A small tremble went through her at the thought of her belly swollen with his child. It wasn't an unpleasant thought, even if she would be doing it to provide Drangar with heirs; heirs who would likely have to fight their cousins for the crown.

"The storm rages on," Hamish said, pulling on his pants.

"It does not. We have a reprieve today." It was true—the worst of the squalls had passed. "And it is light for a few more hours."

"So what do you want to do?" he asked.

"Walk west. I haven't been that way."

"The tracks are poor this time of year, and the wolves will be hunting."

"I'm not scared of wolves."

"Me, neither." He shrugged and touched his shoulder, over his scar. "Just don't like them much."

"Oh, come on, let's go. Or I'll go on my own, *ja*. You stay here."

"No. I'll come with you. We can check the traps down by the river on the way."

She smiled and reached for her tunic. After pulling it on, she wrapped a scarf around her neck then added her fur cloak, fastening it securely with her wolf's-head brooch.

Hamish also dressed warmly, and when they each had secured their weapons, they set a thick log-burner on the fire and went out into the elements.

Hamish ducked his head and headed for the track.

Astrid followed, her feet crunching on the icy ground.

The track held more snow than the beach and had evidence of their tracks over the last few days. But other than hares and birds, nothing else had come their way.

"It's a long walk to the mountains," he said.

"I have made long walks since I was a little girl, from the first years I could walk." She thought of Uppsala. "Nine days, through the forest, over mountains, across valleys, circling great fjords."

"Where were you going?" He glanced at her. "It took nine days?"

Tiny snowflakes sat on his eyebrows and his growing beard. She hoped the snow wouldn't come down heavily again.

"To the sacred grove and Uppsala."

"What is Uppsala?"

A smile spread on her face as she thought of it. "It is a beautiful temple. A place where the gods visit mortals every nine years."

"Like a church?"

"No, it is more than one of your churches. Much more. Yggdrasil, an ancient tree, is so magical, it reaches up into other realms, and as you walk past it, following the golden chains to the temple, you really feel that Odin is there, and Thor, Frey, Freya—all the gods." She pressed her hand to her chest. "They are waiting for sacrifices to be made. They must always be appeased and worshipped. It is in our best interest not to anger them and only be noticed by them for the right reasons."

He held a branch back as she stepped passed it. "What are the golden chains for?"

"Each link signifies a day, each day links to the next. They are all of equal importance because without one, there would be no chain. Every day is important."

"And the sacrifices? Are they animals?"

"Each day, for nine days, there are three sacrifices. Two animals and one human."

"*Human!*"

"*Ja*, a young man who desires to drink with the gods and eat the food the divine chef Andhrímnir provides anew each day is sacrificed."

"You kill a human?"

"*I* don't. The gothi do, and then they hang him in the tree, letting his blood baste the branches."

"That's awful."

"What is?" She stopped and stared at him.

The wind pressed his hood against his chest. "Life is a gift. It shouldn't be taken early."

"They *want* to sacrifice themselves."

"Really?"

"Mostly." She frowned.

"What do you mean?"

"Orm. My father put him forward to be sacrificed and he was accepted. It was a great honor for the family."

"But?"

"But Orm refused. He said he wasn't ready to feast with the gods. My father was furious. He's never forgiven him."

"Your father wanted his own son to die?" His tone was incredulous.

"Hamish, I've told you before, we see death differently to you Christians. Valhalla is a wonderful place full of food and drink, warmth and laughter. There are virgins for the warriors to do with as they please. To be with all the gods is to feel your heart full and your soul complete."

"Have you not had your fill of virgins?" He raised his eyebrows at her as they took the turn toward the river and their traps.

She laughed and squeezed his arm, over his thick cloak. "I always have hunger for my mortal virgin."

He wrapped his arm over her shoulders and pulled her close as they walked. "I'm glad to hear it."

They soon reached the river. It was glacial blue and rushing over rocks, though at this point, it was only knee-deep. It was a place he, Kenna, and Bryce crossed often in the summer. Boar hunting was good on the other side.

"Are they wolf tracks?" Astrid said, peering into the bare-boned shrubbery. "*Ja*, they are."

"Damn," he muttered. "I hope they haven't taken our catch."

She didn't answer but hoped the same. They'd been lucky two days ago and caught a large hare. It had made for a good meal.

Instinctively, she touched the bone handle of her dagger, making sure it was still there. Then she hitched up the quiver of arrows over her shoulder.

They followed the river toward the fall. Should she tell him about the prophecy? Would he believe that her mother and Freya had come to her and said that she would bear him three strong and powerful sons?

Did he even want her to be the mother of his children?

"Hamish?"

"Aye?"

"Do you want children?"

He looked at her, his eyes narrowed against the wind. It was picking up again. "What kind of question is that?"

"It's just a question?" She went for nonchalance.

"I suppose," he said.

"And who do you want to be their mother?"

He stopped, turned fully to her, and frowned. "Are you offering?"

"No! I just wondered if there was a Christian woman in Tillicoulty you had set your sights on as the mother of your children."

"What? Why would you think that? I'm here with you, aren't I?" He set a cool palm over her cheek. "There's no woman in Tillicoulty I have my sights on, not in any other village, either, for that matter. Not in the rest of the world."

She stared into his eyes. His pupils were wide and she felt like she could really see into him.

"Do you have a man in Drangar waiting for you?" he asked quietly.

She huffed. "There are plenty who are hopeful for my return and my affections, but I care so little, I can barely remember their names. I am a princess, remember? Quite the catch."

"Catching you! Not an easy task." He kissed the tip of her cold nose. "I should know."

"You think you have caught me?"

He laughed and carried on walking. "Not a chance. I know you will toss me aside when you bore of me. When you find a Viking with your beliefs and a big cock who promises you more than I can." He paused. "I am a realist."

She fell behind him as the track narrowed beside a steep bank. "My brother has his cock pierced, you know."

"*What?*" Hamish stopped and turned.

She laughed. "*Ja*, a big, silver ring right on the end." She made a circle with her finger.

A flash of horror crossed his eyes. "That must be the most painful thing to endure...the most painful thing that I can think of."

"You don't want to get one, then?"

"No, I bloody well don't."

"Apparently, it adds to female pleasure. Just think what fun your sister must be having." She laughed again.

He shuddered. "I'd rather not think about my sister having sex." He stomped off the path, toward the traps.

"Really?" She paused. "So how do you think I know Haakon has the piercing?"

Hamish froze and looked at her from beneath his hood. "Tell me you have not had sex with your brother."

She shrugged.

"Astrid, that is a great sin."

Such horror flashed in his eyes that she burst out laughing and kicked up a pile of snow.

"*Astrid!*"

"Of course I haven't. I might be a heathen, but I am not twisted."

He raised his eyebrows, indicating that he wasn't so sure.

She laughed harder. "I'm not."

He smiled, through relief, she'd bet. "Tell me, then: how do you know about his piercing?"

"Well, apart from the fact that Haakon is not a shy man, I watched my mother pierce him on his sixteenth summer day."

He shuddered. "Rather him than me. Oh, look..."

A hare had been caught in their trap, and luckily, it was still there.

"Great." She rushed to get it. "This will feed us well tonight."

"Do you still want to go into the mountains?" He looked up at the darkening sky. "We could go back, eat, bathe, fuck…"

"Tempting." She attached the dead hare to her belt, beneath her cloak. "And the next storm is coming quicker than we thought." As she'd spoken, a rumble of thunder filled the darkening sky. "Let's go to the fall. I can sacrifice the hare's guts to the goddess Sága. She must be appeased every winter or in the summer, souls will go over her edge and drown in her depths."

He nodded and took to the track again.

One of the things she liked about Hamish was that he accepted her gods. Not like that annoying priest at the village, Olaf—he was full of his own self-importance, as though he alone spoke to his god in some kind of private conversation.

The river was noisy here. It had narrowed and deepened. A tree hung half over it. For a moment, she wondered what it would be like on a warm summer's day. Calm. Green. Plentiful.

Would she stay long enough to see it?

Ja. If she was to give Hamish three sons. She'd have to.

With a sudden squeeze of her heart, she realized her plans were changing. When she'd marched from Tillicoulty in the middle of the night, her plan had been to make her way home, find sea passage, and return to her father, the only man she loved.

But now… Now she had Hamish.

HAMISH PEERED FORWARD at the expansive view he knew so well. Snow was falling in the distance—a dark-gray haze over the far edge of the mountain range. The river gushed on after it fell, twisting through the scar it had created in the land. The trees were coated in a blanket that made their boughs heavy and to his right, a skein of geese was making for shelter, calling as they went.

"What is that?" Astrid said, squatting at his side and pointing at the very thing that had just turned his blood cold.

"It's King Athol and his men."

"King Athol?" She frowned. "They weren't there before."

"No." His mouth set in a grim line.

"What's he doing here?" She pulled up her hood, trapping her hair within it.

"Nothing good. He usually collects his taxes from the village in the spring. The journey is hard in the winter."

"So why has he made it?"

Hamish studied the small, temporary dwellings. Several spirals of smoke danced upward and he could make out a dozen or so horses. There were a few men scurrying about, but not many. Likely, they were sheltering and waiting for the storm to pass.

"He's come to collect the taxes, hasn't he?" Astrid said. "Early."

"Maybe, but more than that, he has come to reclaim his crown. The one Haakon has taken. He must have heard of it from a wanderer." Hamish blew out a breath. The wind snatched the puff of mist away instantly. "And Haakon is not going to give it back."

"You're right, he's not." She paused. "So he's come for war. King Athol."

"Aye, he's come for a war. A war with Tillicoulty."

"What are you going to do?"

"We have to go and warn them. Warn Haakon and Orm and Noah. And we have to go now."

"What? No." She stood. "I'm not."

Hamish also stood. "We have to. It's the right thing to do."

"No. I said I wouldn't go back there and I'm not." She folded her arms beneath her cloak.

"Well, I am." He frowned at her, appalled at her stubbornness and lack of empathy.

"So go." She shrugged. "Go back."

"Come with me."

"No. You stay here with me." She scowled at him. "They have made their own bed. Let them lie in it and we will lie in ours."

"That is a wicked thing to say about innocent people, Astrid."

Her mouth pursed and her eyes narrowed.

"I cannot agree with you on this," he said. "How can we go back to the cave knowing our families and friends are about to be attacked and we could have warned them?"

"I can."

"Then you are not as loyal a woman as I'd believed."

"What do you know about me? Nothing. That's what. Nothing." She waved her hand in the air flippantly.

"I know plenty."

"You know I have a tight cunny and pert tits, that's all. That's all men ever want to know."

Snatching in a breath, Hamish turned. He marched onto the track, following his own footprints. That last statement didn't deserve a reply. "I have people I love in Tillicoulty," he threw over his shoulder. "I thought you did too."

He kept walking and sent a prayer heavenward that she'd follow. She could be cold and calculating, and she said what she thought without filter, but surely, she would come with him to warn her brothers and fellow Vikings about an imminent invasion. They needed to be prepared. It was the only way they stood a chance.

Invasion. Just the thought injected terror into him. Tillicoulty was a peaceful village full of farmers, not warriors. Yet now, with their new king, a battle was on their doorstep.

But he couldn't quite bring himself to regret the Vikings washing up on their shores. If they hadn't, he'd still have been a virgin waiting for life to happen and his heart wouldn't know what it was like to be with a complex, passionate woman. Her glares could curdle milk, yet her touch was heaven-sent. She was impulsive and intense, her moods flipped from one breath to the next, and he loved that.

He loved *her*.

"Wait!" The thump of her boots behind him. "Wait for me. Tillicoulty is going to need all the warriors and shield-maidens it can get."

He smiled and his heart filled with warmth again. Without Astrid, there'd be an emptiness in his life he wouldn't be able to fill. Without her, there'd be holes in his very soul.

She linked her cool hand with his and nudged him with her shoulder. "I was only jesting with you. Of course I'm coming to Tillicoulty."

"Aye, I know." He chuckled. "I know."

Chapter Fourteen

ASTRID DUCKED BENEATH a low bow and stepped over a snow-covered log, or maybe it was just a mound of earth. It was deep and drifting here, in the forest. The track had not been used and the going was slow. There was still another ten minutes of it before they reached the clearing.

"There're more wolf prints," Hamish said.

She scowled at the large paw marks in the snow. "No sign of any kill. They'll be hungry. That's why they're prowling near to the village."

"It's their way, and why the children are not allowed out of the fort walls in the winter months."

"I hope my brother has made some improvements to the fort walls. Right now, an army of bairns could scale them."

Hamish said nothing and kept on walking, the squeak and crunch of his boots on snow seeming to echo around the tree trunks.

"When do you think King Athol will attack?" she asked, following him.

"I am surprised it is not today. There's no storm."

"It could be there's sickness in the camp. That would be good for us." She stopped. There was movement in the trees above and then the unmistakable *caw, caw* of a raven. "Wait."

"What is it?" Hamish turned, searching the deep shadows as he did so.

"A raven. This is a good omen." She stared up at it.

It cawed again.

"I believe Odin is telling us not to delay," she said, a familiar sense of trepidation and excitement gripping her. It was the way a looming battle always affected her.

"I could not agree with Odin more." Hamish reached for her hand. "Come, let's hurry. I have a bad feeling about this place today." He pressed his fingertips to his cross.

They took two steps, side by side, then Hamish froze.

Astrid did the same.

The slinking shadow up ahead was unmistakable.

Wolf.

"Do you see it?" she whispered, reaching for an arrow.

"Aye. Can you see more?"

"Not yet."

Hamish drew his long dagger. "I hate these bloody things."

"Not my favorite. But at least if there is only one..." She set her arrow in her bow.

"There isn't. Fuck." He half-turned so their backs were against each other's. "I can see another."

"A pack. Damn it. Maybe that was what the raven was telling us."

"Let's hope he helps us out."

The wolf Astrid had in her sights revealed itself a little more. Instinctively, she released her arrow. It flew between the tree trunks dead straight and hit its target on the shoulder.

The wolf whimpered and in a flurry of snow, it disappeared.

"I got it," she said. "Not dead, but hopefully, it will take itself off to lick its wounds."

"Good shot." He nudged her with his shoulder. "Reckon you can get this one? I'd rather not wait until it's near enough for me to get it with the sword."

They moved around and she spotted the wolf he was talking about. It was bigger than the other one, darker too, meaning it had an advantage in the dense forest.

"I'll try," she said, priming an arrow and taking aim.

The raven cawed, as though Odin himself were encouraging her.

She closed one eye, again took aim, and then fired.

The arrow partially disappeared in the shadows, but then a satisfying *whump* and a yelp told her she'd been successful again.

"Well done," he said, turning and grinning at her. "You're an incredible shot. Not many could have gotten both of them in this light."

She half-shrugged, even though she glowed with pride at the praise. "It was easy."

He chuckled softly and pressed his cool lips to hers. "Come on. Let's keep going."

Suddenly, there was a rush of movement to his right. A wolf leapt from the undergrowth, teeth bared, claws out, and hackles raised.

"Hamish!" she screamed.

He turned, raising his sword, ready for attack. But the wolf was close and already flying through the air. Its huge paws landed on Hamish, sending him off-balance. He fell backward onto his ass, sword ready.

The snarling wolf went for his arm. Hamish swiped at it, catching its neck. But this just seemed to anger it more and it went back again in a rage of fur, claws, and teeth.

Astrid had her dagger drawn.

"No!" Hamish shouted. "Stay away."

"But…"

He grunted and twisted, then jumped to his feet, his cloak staying on the snowy earth having come undone.

Drool dripped from the wolf's sharp front teeth and it went in again, leaping into the air, its claws at the ready.

Hamish stooped down and angled his sword at the wolf's chest. By the time the wolf realized its mistake, it was too late. It plunged onto the sharp weapon, surprise in its eyes as it let out a howl.

Hamish made a low, growling sound as the body dropped onto him, knocking him back to the floor. Its life-blood stained the snow around them bright scarlet.

"Hamish!" Astrid rushed up to him. "Are you hurt?"

He didn't answer.

"Hamish!" Panic gripped her. What if he was hurt? Dead? Maybe the wolf had managed to deliver a fatal bite or the sword had twisted and punctured his heart?

"Oh, please. No." She dragged at the lifeless wolf. It was heavy and she heaved and grunted.

Suddenly, it moved, not by itself, but because Hamish was shoving at it.

"Fuck, Hamish. You scared me there. I thought..."

"You thought I was dead." His blood-splattered face appeared. "It'd take more than a damn wolf to do that." He grunted and freed himself from the big animal, tipping it onto its side and creating another gush of blood from its chest.

He stood and pulled his sword free of the carcass.

"Fuck," she said, looking down at it. "You have crazy-brave wolves here."

He wiped the blood from his sword on a patch of snow. He was breathing hard. "We should get going."

"*Ja*, we really should." She was searching him for signs of bites or claw marks. "Are you sure you're unharmed?"

He cupped her cheek. "Would take more than a wolf to finish me off."

She raised her eyebrows. That had been a pretty close call. If he'd been alone and all three had attacked, it might have been a different story.

"I grew up here," he said. "I understand my homeland as you understand yours."

"So what would finish you off?" she asked.

His eyes were bright, his body still charged for a fight. "Losing you," he said briskly. "If anything happened to you, I wouldn't be able to keep on living. What kind of world would it be if you weren't walking in it?"

Before Astrid could think of a smart remark, she was being tugged through the forest, Hamish holding her hand tightly as he marched forward on a track she couldn't see.

He couldn't live without her?

Was he speaking the truth?

They passed by a small stream, a tree that had been struck by lightning and lost its pines, and a huge rock that had a streak of shiny, white stone going through it.

"Are we nearly there?" she asked.

"Aye, not far now." He glanced over his shoulder. "With a bit of luck, the wolf pack will prey on King Athol while he sleeps."

"We wouldn't be that lucky."

"True."

Finally, as darkness seeped over the land, the fort of Tillicoulty came into view like a shadow looming in the distance. The clearing before it was devoid of snow, as though many men had been marching there. A dog roamed around, sniffing.

"Not where we'd planned to go today," she said, tightening her bow over her shoulder. "Or ever again."

"It's good fortune that you suggested we walk." He kept on going, ground-eating paces now that the snow wasn't a hindrance.

"We'll go straight to Haakon," she said.

"No, I will tell my father first."

"Haakon is your king, Hamish."

"Aye, but my father is my father. Kings come and go."

She frowned. "That is treason."

He laughed. "You would tell your father before Haakon if we were in Drangar."

"*Ja*, I would."

"Who goes there?" a voice shouted down from the watchtower. "Announce yourself or prepare for my arrow in your heart."

"Brother! Is that you?" Astrid called, speeding up.

"Astrid?" Orm yelled.

She could make out his outline. Like her, he had a bow on his back and his hood was pulled up tight. "*Ja*, it's me."

"And Hamish?" Orm shouted.

"Aye." Hamish lifted a hand. "Open the gates. Let us in. We have important information and there is no time to waste."

"I'll get them," Gunner called.

Soon, they were splashing through the muddy puddle at the base of the gate. "There has been much movement today," Hamish said, glancing down. "Lots of people coming and going."

"Haakon has been teaching combat to the farmers," Gunner said. "They have lots of practice ahead of them, but it's a good start."

"They do not have time to practice," Hamish said with a grunt as he made his way toward his family home.

"What?" Orm said, skipping along at his side. "What did you say?"

"Come with me," he said. "Make sure there is someone on the watchtower, though. You need to hear this, and you, Gunner."

Astrid looked at the determined set of Hamish's jaw as he walked past a basket glowing with fire. She'd gotten used to gentle Hamish, her lover, a man with whom she swapped sagas and secrets, yet here he was, all confident and dominant, and she found she liked that side of him too—a lot.

"Haakon should hear it," Orm said. "He is king."

"I am going to my father," Hamish said with a glance at Orm, as though challenging him to argue. "But you can get King Haakon to join us."

"You go to Great House," Gunner said. "Now."

"No, the king can come to us. It is Astrid and I who have the information he needs and I must see my parents."

"Information? About what?" Orm twisted his hands together the way he did when excited for news.

"Information about King Athol and his men." Hamish paused at the entrance of his home. "And how long the king has until they arrive here in Tillicoulty."

"They are here?" Orm's eyes widened. The kohl he always wore had run down his cheeks like black tears.

"They are close," Astrid said. "We have seen them this day."

"The All-Seeing Father is very wise," Orm said with a grin. "And you being gone for so long is a good omen, I said it was. I knew you would return with new wisdom of this land."

"It is not a wisdom you want, to know you are going to be attacked." Astrid frowned.

"It is exactly what we must know." Orm rubbed his hands together in fast, sharp movements.

"Where were you?" Gunner directed at Astrid. "All that time."

"I was away, that's all. Away from you stupid idiots with your ridiculous faces and your annoying questions."

"Astrid," Hamish said. "We haven't got time to waste." He ducked into his home.

"He's right." She tilted her chin. "Go, both of you. Go and get the king—now."

"Hamish!" a woman's voice shrieked. "In God's name, where have you been? And where are you hurt?"

Astrid followed Hamish into his home. She'd never been in this round, turf-roofed dwelling before, but it was much like the others. A fire in the center, cots around the edge, an area for preparing and storing food and a weaving loom with a small, wooden stool. There were several carvings and crosses on the wall along with a decorative tapestry of a tree, an apple, and a mostly naked man and woman.

Hamish's mother was pulling his cloak from him and flapping

around like a worried hen.

"I am unhurt, Mother. It is wolf blood," Hamish said.

"Wolf. Oh, dear Lord." She rushed to wet a rag, twisting it in a clean bowl of water. "The wolves are the devil's work, and they come closer and closer."

"Son." Noah stood and leaned heavily on his cane. "I'm glad you have returned. But you have a sense of urgency about you. What is it?"

"King Athol, Father." Hamish allowed his mother to wipe the bloodstains from his cheek, though he barely seemed to notice what she was doing. "He is in a clearing beneath the fall, not half a day's walk from here."

Noah frowned. "This time of year? He is collecting taxes in the snow?"

"He is not here to collect taxes," Astrid said. "He is here to reclaim his crown."

Noah frowned and sat back down. "Astrid, it is good to see you."

"It is?" She raised her eyebrows.

"Aye, I was worried. This is a strange land for you, and as you have no doubt seen, the wolves are brave when their bellies are so empty."

Astrid studied his kind, old eyes. He appeared to be speaking the truth. He was glad she'd returned safely. "I...I... You do not need to concern yourself with my wellbeing."

Noah looked at her steadily for a moment then switched his attention back to his son.

"That will do, Mother. Thank you," Hamish said, moving from the wet cloth.

"I will get you warm ale," Fion said.

"And for Astrid?"

"Of course."

"What is happening?" Haakon suddenly appeared, his face a little flushed and his cape scrunched around his neck as though thrown on in a hurry. "Sister."

"Brother." She scowled at him. "Are you still a Christian?"

He chuckled and drew her into a hug. "I am thankful to all the gods who look over us that you have returned."

His embrace was tight and warm and familiar and she closed her eyes for a moment, glad suddenly that she was seeing him again, even though she'd planned never to.

"Hamish. You have returned." Kenna ducked into the building and looked from Hamish to his bloody tunic. "Wolves?"

"Aye." He half-shrugged. "But that is not our story."

"So tell us," Fion said, finishing handing out ale.

"So what is?" Kenna asked, reaching for her mother's hand and squeezing it in both of hers.

A pang went through Astrid. It was the kind of gesture she'd have done, and had done, when her mother had been alive. Hamish was lucky; he had a kind family full of people who loved each other.

"King Athol and his men are here," Astrid said, looking up at her brother. "They are camped only a few hours' walk from here, hunkering down while the storms rage, but the first chance they get, expect a visit."

Haakon frowned, his thick eyebrows coming together.

"That is sooner than expected," Astrid said.

"But we will be ready." Haakon looked at Hamish and then Noah. "I promised to defend Tillicoulty when I became king, and I will."

"Aye, we will." Orm appeared, Gunner and Knud with him. "Though there is much to be done. We must build a hidden ditch, a spike gate, organize the piles of boulders on the ramparts so we can drop them on assailants, and—"

"*Ja*, Orm." Haakon nodded. "We must do all of that."

"And it will have to be done in dark hours," Hamish said. "There is no time to waste." He took a sip of his warm ale.

Astrid did the same with hers, glad of the fragrant warmth slipping down her throat.

"You're right," Haakon said. "If we are going to rid ourselves of this man who unjustly demands money, then we must throw all our energies into being prepared."

"It's just a shame you have no warriors or shield-maidens." Astrid downturned her mouth.

"That is not true." Kenna frowned at her.

"It is true." Astrid shrugged.

"The men and women of the village show strength and skill and a willingness to learn," Haakon said. "We have practiced shield walls, and the archers are a keen shot. We have the makings of an army."

"I thank you for sharing your knowledge with my fellow villagers." Hamish stood and walked up to Haakon. He clamped his hand on his shoulder. "King Haakon."

"And I thank you for bringing my sister back to Tillicoulty."

Before Astrid could respond, Hamish laughed. "Oh, I didn't. She came of her own free will. I know her well enough to understand that your sister does *everything* of her own free will. She cannot be persuaded or cajoled if she does not want to do something."

"That is true." Haakon chuckled.

Orm clapped and laughed. "I know what has happened. I know what has happened." He pointed between Astrid and Hamish with a grin of glee. "You two have been—"

"Shut the fuck up," Astrid snapped at him.

"But it is the path the gods have set you on," Orm continued. "What your runestones predicted. Your destiny is—"

"I said, *shut it*. Orm."

He wouldn't be persuaded to stop gabbling on. "The runestones said it, many years ago, Astrid, you must remember. You threw Freya's Wunjo stone, eight, and it predicted passion and love after a journey of great change and a man who—"

Her anger swelled. That runestone reading was the last thing she wanted her brother yapping on about. She stepped up to him and sloshed her warm ale into his face. "May Thor strike you dead, Orm, because if you keep talking, you'll wish you were."

He stopped mid-sentence, eyes wide, drink dripping from his nose and chin.

She glared at him.

"Maybe I'm not so glad you are back," Orm said, licking the ale from his lips and frowning. "You are a pain in the ass, Astrid."

Chapter Fifteen

"WE WILL START now," Haakon said. "There is much to be done, and only the gods know when the weather will turn and Athol will attack."

"What do you want me to do?" Noah asked, kissing the cross at his neck.

"You have pains in your knees, Noah," Haakon said with a frown. "Stay by the fire. Perhaps you should pray to God."

"I can do that, but I want to help. Please give me a task."

Haakon hesitated, then, "Organize for boulders to be piled up on the ramparts. We will use these as missiles should anyone try to climb up."

"I can help with that," Hamish's mother said. "And some of the older children will also help."

"Mother, it is wet and cold outside and…" Kenna shook her head worriedly.

"I want to help too. Let me do this."

"But—"

"Kenna," Hamish said. "Everyone has something to offer our cause. Let Mother help, if that is her wish."

Kenna glanced at her husband and then nodded at Fion. "Yes, you are right. And the king and I thank you."

"Orm, organize for a spike fence to be constructed," Haakon said. "We will lay it flat and conceal it with foliage and then raise it rapidly if they charge. Ensure it has sturdy ropes attached to do this and men who can work it quickly."

Orm nodded and slipped from the dwelling, still wiping ale from his face. Good. Astrid was glad he'd gone.

"Shall I gather men to dig a ditch?" Gunner said.

"*Ja*, you do that with Knud and Egil. I am going to speak to Hywel and have him get straight to work on more weapons and shields. Ivar can help him."

"What can I do?" Hamish asked, tickling Lass behind the ears. She'd sneaked in and curled around his legs.

"Eat, warm up, and then help with the ditch or make more arrows." He glanced at Astrid. "You have done us a great service by bringing this information."

The small home emptied quickly, though the sense of urgency and determination lingered.

Except for Lass, who flopped onto her bed of straw.

Hamish walked to the fire and dipped a ladle into a pot of steaming broth. "Do you want some?"

Astrid's stomach rumbled. "*Ja*, I'm hungry."

"It's pork."

She nodded and then washed her hands and sat. She watched Hamish moving around, breaking bread and pouring ale. This was his home and she liked how comfortable he was in it.

"Haakon has many ideas," Hamish said, handing her a bowl of food and a spoon.

"He has been to battle more times than he can count. Led in battle too, though then he had his twin brother, Ravn, at his side."

"And they were victorious?"

"Of course." She took a mouthful of the rich, meaty broth. "The gods look on my brothers with favor."

Hamish was quiet.

"What is it?" she asked, dipping bread into her food.

"If lives are lost, then I can't help but think we'll regret not paying

King Athol's taxes. Money is worth less than life. Gold coins can be replaced."

"But to be oppressed is to live a life as a thrall and is that life worth living?"

He said nothing.

"Hamish." She leaned forward. "To live free is worth fighting for. To die defending your people is a sacrifice worth making." She studied him. "It is the honorable thing to do."

"I would give my life in a heartbeat for my family and for my people." He narrowed his eyes. "And I'd die for you without a moment's hesitation."

Warmth spread through her as she looked into his eyes.

"You should not forget that," he said.

"It is you who forgets. I am a shield-maiden. I can defend myself."

"Aye, but I want you to know how I feel."

"Which is?"

"I will always be on your side, Astrid."

"That is good for you, because not being on my side would make life very dangerous for you."

He chuckled softly and carried on eating.

The meal was good and the tender meat full of flavor. Outside, the village was busy with shouted instructions and loud hammering. Dogs, unused to the evening hustle and bustle, barked. Lass jumped up and ran out to join in the activity.

"We should help now," Hamish said after wiping out the bowls and setting them on a shelf. "There is much to do."

"In a few minutes." She stood and went to him, wrapping her arms around his torso and resting her cheek on his wide back.

He turned and embraced her. Set a kiss on her brow. "Tell me about Freya's Wunjo stone."

"It is just a stone." She prickled. "Orm had no right to talk of it."

"Aye, it is," he said lightly. "Just a stone."

She was glad he didn't press her. But Hamish knew the stones were important, so he was wise not to push for more information. Perhaps she'd tell him one day. Maybe she wouldn't.

"Fuck me," she said, then she swiped her lips over his. "Fuck me now. Here. I want it. I want you."

The right side of his mouth twitched. "When there is so much to do?"

"We will not be missed for a while."

"What if my parents come back?" He raised his eyebrows and drew her nearer. His cock was already stiffening and prodded her hip.

"Then they will see that their son is a man and not a boy virgin."

He chuckled then squeezed her ass cheeks over her pants. "It would probably be better to tell them rather than show them, but…"

"But what?" She reached for his belt buckle.

"But, aye, let's fuck."

She kissed him hungrily and dragged at his belt and pants, freeing his hardening cock. It was going to be different this time. She'd thought of it on their walk to the village, she'd planned it as they'd eaten.

And she was excited for it.

He freed her pants and shoved at them, his breaths quickening. She helped the pants on their way and pushed them over her boots, kicking them aside.

"You get hard so quick," she said, clasping his cock in her fist.

He groaned and scooped her up, lifting her high and kissing her with a desperate urgency.

Her pussy pressed against the hair above his cock and she wrapped her bare legs around his hips, crossing her ankles.

Three big paces and her back was against the wall and his cock was prodding her entrance. They'd done it so many times now, but it never got boring. He always had her desperate for it, the rest of the world fading away.

"Hamish." She held his face, stared into her eyes. His cock tip was kissing her pussy. Wide and hot and ready. "Fuck me, fuck me so damn hard."

He gritted his teeth, then curling his hips and holding her tightly, he blasted in to full depth.

The sudden, fierce invasion created a stitch of pain in her pussy and she cried out.

"Sorry," he gasped, stilling.

"No, no, don't stop. I want it like this. Hamish...fuck me hard."

He grunted and pulled back a little, then stormed in again to full depth.

The air was knocked from her lungs and she clung to him, taking it all and pressing to him.

"Astrid," he gasped against her lips. "I want you to come."

"I will." She rolled her body against his, stimulating her nub. "Just fuck me, hard, harder."

He blasted in again, shunting her up the wall. "Like that?"

"*Ja*, like that. Oh, in the name of all the gods, oh, like that." She held him tighter. "More. Give me more."

He gave it, thrusting into her, his cock a spear driving into her pussy and his body taking possession of hers. It was feral and primitive. He hadn't been this rough with her before and seeing his passion, his desire for her in its raw state, was intoxicating.

Soon, the pressure was mounting and growing in her nub. She wanted to come like this, while he was driving in and out of her with feral passion. It was as if he had only a tenuous grip on control.

"Hamish," she gasped, grabbing his ear and pulling. "Come with me."

"You come first," he said onto her lips. His stubbled chin scraped against hers. "Come. For. Me."

"I want to come...*with* you."

He moaned and closed his eyes. "God, I'm close but...no, you come."

"Hamish. Come with me."

He opened his eyes, staring at her as he tunneled into her, pausing balls-deep. "I'll have to pull out…soon." His cheeks were flushed, his eyes flashing with need and desire. "Really soon."

"Come inside me," she said, scraping her hands into his thick hair. "Come inside me. I want your seed."

"You want my seed? But…?"

"Just do it, Hamish." She clenched her pussy around him. "Come inside me, like this, high inside me."

"Oh, God, I'm going to…" His mouth slammed down on hers and he thrust wildly, filling her, pushing her closer.

She loved it, knowing that he wasn't going to withdraw this time. That he was going to give himself entirely, and hopefully the first of her sons too.

"Oh, don't stop!" She wailed. "Don't stop."

If his parents walked in and saw them like this, they'd be shocked. They'd know she'd corrupted their pure son to the very core of his soul. He was a changed man. A man who knew what it was to seek and find pleasure. To understand the needs of his body and of a woman's body. Maybe they'd say she'd tainted him, dirtied him, debased him, but Astrid didn't care. Hamish was perfect like this.

He was perfect for her.

"Oh, fuck…" He gasped, gripping her ass cheeks so hard, it hurt. But she reveled in the discomfort, mixing it with all the other sensations that were besieging her.

"I'm coming…" She gasped, closing her eyes and capturing the moment the pressure became almost too much to bear. "Oh…yes…that's it…"

He stayed with her, pounding hard, rubbing her nub with his body as his cock went deep, deep and deeper still over and over.

She wailed.

He cried out.

And then she was coming, spasming around his throbbing cock as he emptied his release into her.

They were kissing wildly as their bodies pulsed and slicked and sent wings of pleasure racing through their veins.

Wrapping her arms around his shoulders, she pulled him closer. At this moment, she couldn't imagine ever letting him go. She didn't want to not have him inside of her.

He was panting as he continued to rub up against her, eking out every bit of her pleasure just the way she liked. She'd taught him well.

"Hamish," she gasped, her lips moving against his. "That was good. So good."

"But why did you...?" He pulled back a fraction. A frown creased his brow. "You always insist I pull out, that I don't release my seed inside you, so what—?"

"I want your sons." She touched his cheek. "I want your sons in my belly, Hamish."

His eyes widened. "You do?"

"Ja." She paused. "Why? Don't you want me to carry your heirs?"

"Aye, of course I do. You are the only person I would want to carry my children, Astrid. You must know that."

She didn't know that, so she said nothing.

"But why now?" He hesitated, as though wondering whether or not to push her. "What has made you change your mind?"

"It doesn't matter."

"Aye, it does. My cock and my seed are deep inside you. You've just told me you want my sons. Talk to me, Astrid. I deserve to know what's made you change your mind about me coming inside your sweet body."

She huffed. It was clear this time, he wasn't going to let it go. "It was a prophecy?" She scowled, waiting for him to dismiss it.

"Go on."

"It came to me. Well, actually, my mother and Freya, the goddess herself, came to me."

He nodded slowly and adjusted his grip on her ass. It seemed he had no intention of withdrawing and putting her down to the floor to have this conversation. "And what did they say, your mother and the goddess Freya? What was the prophecy?"

She gritted her teeth and closed her eyes. It had been so real. It *was* so real to her. "That I will give you three flame-haired sons who will be the rightful heirs to Drangar and who will finish my father's work."

He raised his eyebrows. "You will give me three sons?"

"*Ja.* Three pagan sons."

"Not Christian?"

"No." She glared at him.

He nodded slowly.

"And our sons will appease the gods. They will be brave and wise and skilled warriors," she said.

"I like them already." His mouth twitched into a half-smile and his eyes sparkled in the low lighting.

"I'm being serious." She frowned. "The prophecy is a truth and a good omen."

"I am also being serious." He tipped his head closer and spoke onto her lips. "If we have made the first of our sons tonight, I will protect him and teach him to be a man you'll be proud of. I swear I will do that for all of our sons, and daughters should we be lucky enough to have them too."

Her heart squeezed as she gazed into his eyes and saw only truth and honor.

"Whether he is Christian or not it will not matter to me, Astrid," he went on. "For my God loves everyone, and sees the good in everyone. He will love our children and walk with them every step of their lives." He paused and a muscle danced in his jawline. "As I wish to walk with you for the rest of my life."

"Do you know what you are saying?"

"Aye. I do not wish to be parted from you. I wish to start and end each of my days with you until my final breath."

"What if I go to Drangar with our sons?"

Hamish wouldn't leave Lothlend and she'd have to prepare herself for that. Prepare herself for disappointment and loneliness when they'd been two emotions she'd had a reprieve from.

"Then I will come with you to Drangar. I will row alongside you. I will fight any wolf or bear that gets in our way."

She nodded, not trusting herself to speak.

"And I will fight your brother Ravn if he disrespects you or is a threat to our sons." He kissed the tip of her nose. "I am yours, as I wish you to be mine. Nothing else matters."

"'Nothing else matters'?"

"No." Gently, he lifted her up and his cock slipped from her. He cupped her cheeks. "You are all that matters."

She swallowed tightly, emotions bubbling, then pushed him away. "Put your cock away before someone comes in." She reached for her pants with a slick of moisture coating her upper thighs. "And make sure you're hard at night's end. We should fuck again."

"Aye, Princess, I can do that." He gave her a wink, then reached for his dagger. "Come on, let's go lend a hand."

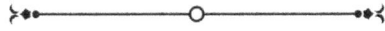

Chapter Sixteen

"**N**OT LIKE THAT, like this." Orm scraped his long dagger up a wooden pole and curls of shavings flew from the end. "Make it a point, sharp, so sharp, like a snake fang. You see?"

Several farmers nodded and carried on working on the spikes for the rising defense. Orm strutted between them, his darkly rimmed eyes alive with excitement and purpose and an amused smile tilting his lips.

"Do you need help?" Hamish asked, surveying the spikes that had already been made. They were a little uneven in size, but not enough to matter.

"Do we look like we need help?" Orm threw his seax into the air. It span twice, then he caught it by the handle.

"I don't know. It's why I'm asking," Hamish said.

Orm pointed at his workers. "No, they are fast learners. They make spikes as well as they now hold a shield wall."

"What's shield wall?" Hamish asked.

"Bloody hell, you have a lot to learn, Christian boy." Astrid rolled her eyes. She was standing beneath a large, iron basket that was aflame to provide light to the busy village now that the sun had gone down, and it caressed her somewhat-mussed-up hair—lingering evidence of their recent passion.

"So tell me, Astrid," Hamish said. They walked away from Orm, who was barking more instructions as he began to unroll ropes. "What is a shield wall?"

"It's a way to defend your warriors from attack yet still allows you to attack. Everyone packs in tight, holds up their shields, and the crossbows fire from the back. When the enemy advances they are first shot with arrows and then spears and then finally swords, by which point the shield wall can dissipate and finish off the last of the attackers."

"It sounds very…organized."

"You don't think it works?" she asked.

"I am sure it does if everyone can hold their nerve."

"Vikings can. It's yet to be seen if your people can."

Hamish glanced around. Usually, at this time of day, at this time of year, everyone would be in their homes or in the Great House. The women would be weaving and cooking, the men drinking and talking. Perhaps the carpenter or ironsmith would be working, but it was a low time of year. Yet now… With Tillicoulty ablaze with light and a hub of productivity, it was as though he'd been dropped into another world.

If it hadn't been because a battle was on the horizon, he'd have enjoyed it.

"There's Kenna," Astrid said. "She appears to be practicing her fighting skills with other village women."

Hamish spotted his sister and several others—young, fit women—wielding short, wooden swords as they mock-fought by the barn.

"They have never raised a sword in defense of their village?" Astrid asked.

"No."

"Only against wolves if out hunting?"

"Aye, likely that. Kenna, yes, she's…special, but not many of the others."

"They are as inexperienced as babes just off their mother's breasts." Astrid tutted. "They will be easy targets for King Athol's men."

"So go show them how to fight." He turned to face her. "Go show them how shield-maidens fight. Solve the problem."

A line had formed over her brow and she was nibbling on her bottom lip. "I fear they are a lost cause. It is too late."

He raised his eyebrow. "I would have believed you to be a good teacher, Astrid."

She withdrew her sword. "I am." She thought about it and he stayed quiet, letting her mull it over. Then, "I will show them the basics at least, then I won't have it on my conscience when they are all slain in the mud."

Swinging her sword, she stomped off, her shoulders stiff.

A shiver of dread went through him, the word *slain* running over itself in his head. He didn't want to see any villagers slain, least of all women, his friends, his sister…Astrid.

No, Astrid could fend for herself. Couldn't she?

And Kenna had been a good opponent when he and Bryce had practiced with her over the years. She was fast and could dodge almost as quickly as he could blink. But to see her up against one of King Athol's big brutes… No, that didn't bear thinking about.

And no amount of praying would protect her.

He glanced at the watchtower. To the left of it, a steady stream of rocks was being chain-passed up to the rampart by women and children on the cusp of adulthood. To the right of the watchtower, several men were bolstering a weak point.

He wandered through the village, past a coup of clucking chickens who were cross that their evening peace had been disrupted, and a pen of pigs snuffling by their fence in the hope of scraps.

Bryce was still on the watchtower, marching this way and that and peering from his hood.

"Hey," Hamish called up. "Want me to take over?"

"I am on my watch for a while longer," Bryce called down. "Then Noah is taking over and I will help dig the ditch with Haakon."

Hamish glanced through the gates. Several fires glowed, illuminating a group of men digging frantically. To the far left was Haakon, Knud, Egil, and Gunner. They were easy to spot, with their height and width. Gunner had removed his cloak and tunic and dug with a bare upper torso despite the winter chill.

Hamish walked over to them, ready to pick up a shovel and join the task.

Haakon saw him approaching and paused, wiping his brow on his forearm.

"What can I do to help?" Hamish asked.

Haakon stooped, picked up a shovel, and tossed it through the air.

Hamish caught it with a snatch of his hand.

"Come dig with us. We need to go deeper but not wider."

Striding forward, Hamish let his cloak land beside several others then drove the shovel into the wet ground.

"Where is Astrid?" Haakon asked as he dug.

"She's with Kenna and the other women, showing them the ways of shield-maidens."

"A task she is well capable of." Haakon huffed as his shovel hit a rock. He reached for it and tossed it aside.

"She is a very capable woman," Hamish said.

Haakon paused and looked at Hamish. "What is there between you and my sister?"

"Does it matter?" Did it? Would Haakon object? He'd stand his ground if so.

"I'm her brother. Of course it matters."

"I care about her. A lot." Hamish gritted his teeth.

"You are one of a long list of fools, then." Haakon chuckled and tossed a pile of earth to one side.

Hamish felt his hackles rise. He didn't like the thought of lots of men lining up for Astrid, past or present, and he also liked to think he was different to the ones before. "I have never considered myself to be foolish."

"Neither did any of her Northland suitors."

"But they weren't enough for her," Hamish said, working on a new patch of earth. "Otherwise, she wouldn't have come with you. She wouldn't have left her home."

"That is true, my friend. There was no one who could withstand her bark. They were always flinching and waiting for the bite."

"She doesn't bite…much."

Haakon chuckled. "Did you fuck her? I'm guessing you've been with her the entire time she's been away."

"That's a personal question."

Haakon stopped digging and leaned on the end of his shovel with his forearms crossed. He studied Hamish. "As I said, she's my sister, so this *is* personal." He paused. "And I'm curious. I bet she does bite, a lot, when she's fucking."

Hamish felt his cheeks redden and a prickle of heat went over his scalp that had nothing to do with exertion. He carried on digging. The crude comment didn't deserve a reply.

"You going to marry her?" Haakon asked, also resuming his task.

"What do you think?"

"I have no idea. That's why I asked."

"She won't marry a Christian."

"Do you know that for sure?" Haakon asked.

"Aye." Hamish felt his neck and jaw tense even further. "I do."

"So you asked her?"

"No, I suppose I'm not as foolish as you seem to think I am."

Haakon said nothing. Instead, he paused and glanced around, as though checking for signs of King Athol and his men sneaking from the forest. "So how do you know for certain she won't marry you?"

"She made it quite clear that I was not marriage material." But he *was* father material. He thought of how she'd told him only minutes ago that she wanted his children. His sons. Three of them. Should he mention that to Haakon? Say it to prove that there was something special between himself and Haakon's complex, feral, intense sister? No, it seemed like a betrayal of Astrid's trust and that was something he held far too precious to risk. He got the feeling once a person lost her trust, it was gone forever.

"We have very different sisters," Haakon said, resuming his work.

"But they are both flesh and blood." Hamish glanced at the fort entrance. "And Astrid is a more experienced warrior than Kenna. I have seen the scar on her arm from a battle near Drangar."

"*Ja*, that was a bloody day." Haakon shook his head. "Terrible day, but at least we were victorious."

"Kenna has never been to battle. She's only sparred with Bryce and myself. With wooden swords."

"There is a first time for everything."

"This could be a first and last time for her, Haakon. You do know that, right?"

Haakon grunted as he whacked the shovel into the ground. "We will pray to your God and make sacrifices to Odin and Thor that we are triumphant and our people's blood does not soak into this earth."

"I thought he was *your* God now?"

"He is." Again, Haakon wiped his forearm over his brow. "But it will be good sense to have all the gods on our side."

Hamish nodded and moved a rock from the earth. "Astrid will fight when the time comes."

"*Ja*, she will not be stopped, not by anyone. And we will be glad to have her skills."

"I do not want her to," Hamish said, "I'm going to tell her as much. And I do not want my sister to fight, either."

Gunner, who had been digging next to them, let out a great, deep guffaw.

"What?" Hamish glared at him.

"When you tell Astrid she can't fight, let me know. I want to watch her tear you to shreds."

144

Hamish felt heat rise on his temples. "She will not tear me to shreds."

"She will." Haakon didn't laugh. He shook his head and down-turned his mouth. "She is a shield-maiden. Nothing will stop her fighting for what she believes in."

"But she doesn't even want to stay in Tillicoulty. Why would she die for it?"

"There is obviously something here she thinks is worth fighting for." Haakon shrugged, though his gaze stayed on Hamish.

Hamish glanced over his shoulder, through the open gates to where the women were still practicing their sword skills. Astrid was in full flow, her sword flying through the air as she demonstrated a duck-and-weave move that resulted in what would have been a lethal kidney blow to an opponent. She was good, he knew that. But would his prayers be answered and see her safely through the battle?

"Kenna shouldn't fight," Hamish said. "As her husband and king, you should forbid it."

"What?" Haakon's eyes widened as he stared at Hamish. "First off, as your king, you should really consider how you address me. You might be my wife's brother, but I am still in charge here."

Hamish frowned and gripped the handle of his shovel tighter.

"And secondly, we need all the shield-maidens we can get."

"Kenna is not a shield-maiden, not like Astrid, and besides…what if she is already carrying your child, your heir? Have you thought of that, Your Grace?" His jaw tensed and he sucked in air, glad of its cooling effect on his temper. "What if you lose not just her, but also a son?"

"It is a risk I must take, the same as you must." Haakon glared at him. "For what if my sister is carrying *your* child?"

"She is not." Hamish looked at the earth and stabbed at it again. "How do you know?"

The truth was Hamish didn't know for sure. He'd spilled his seed into her twice now. His child could have been growing in her belly.

Haakon ducked his head to look at Hamish's face. "You mean you didn't—"

"I don't want to talk about it. It's disrespectful. God has taught me that women are precious and should be protected and revered. It is clearly not how you see them."

"You couldn't be more wrong," Haakon said. "I too believe women should be respected and cherished. I just have a different way of doing that."

"By letting them fight? Take on men who are twice their size and strength?"

"No, by letting them make their own decisions. Both my wife and my sister are intelligent, stubborn, headstrong, and skilled. They are all the qualities of a warrior and they know it. To oppress a woman would anger the goddess Freya, and that is not something I want."

"Again, you talk of your gods." Hamish scowled.

"'Haps there are things you could learn from them." Haakon huffed. "And one of them is not to underestimate a woman just because she is of slight frame and tastes of sweet honey."

Hamish licked his lips and thought of Astrid's taste upon his tongue.

"My friend." Haakon suddenly clasped his shoulder. "Say your prayers and fight well. That is all we can do because King Athol will be coming to us, and he will not be happy that I have a crown he believes is his to wear."

Chapter Seventeen

THE LUR SOUNDED at dawn. A loud trumpeting that had a rush of energy bursting into Astrid's veins.

She sat upright, eyes wide, and stared at the doorway to the small, unoccupied dwelling she'd claimed as her own when she'd first arrived in Tillicoulty.

"What is it?" Hamish asked, also sitting and rubbing his eyes.

"It is a call for warriors." She jumped from their bed. "We are under attack."

"Athol is here?"

"He is the one most likely to be attacking us, *ja*." Quickly, she dressed in pants, boots, and tunic. Then she threw on a fitted, leather corset patterned to look like scales and tightened the laces. It would offer some protection. Next she pulled on a tasset—a war skirt—that flared at her hips. She added a matching leather pauldron to shield her shoulders and tightened the straps over her chest in a cross.

Hamish was also dressing with speed and adding tough leather armor over his clothes. His hair was messy from their lovemaking the night before and he plonked a metal helmet on that had a length of steel to protect his nose.

Still the lur sounded.

"We should go," Astrid said, gathering her hair and tying it back with a strip of leather. "Haakon will be waiting for us." She banged her own helmet on.

"Astrid." Hamish circled his arm around her waist and pulled her close. "I don't want…"

"What?"

His eyes were narrowed and a tendon flexed in his cheek as he stared down at her face.

"Do not tell me not to fight." Irritation clawed at her. There was a fire inside of her chest.

"I wouldn't dare." His lips pressed together. "But fight with all your skill. I don't want to go to this bed tonight without you at my side."

She pulled in a breath, seeing the love and devotion in his eyes. "And I say the same to you." She touched his cheek. "Fight hard and win, for it is not our time to sup from curved horns in the company of the gods, not yet. I have your sons to birth."

He gently touched her stomach over the leather. "The first of which could be in your womb now."

"That thought will make me fight even harder." She reached up and swept her lips over his. "Do not fear. We will lie down together tonight with blood in our veins and breath in our lungs."

He nodded, though his movements were tense and sharp.

"We will champion," she said, reaching for her sword and shield and then tucking her seax into her belt. "The gods are with us. Odin, Thor, and Tyr too."

"Who is Tyr?"

"The God of War," she said, ducking out of the dwelling and into the misty morning. "He sacrificed his hand to chain up the wolf Fenrir; he is honorable and just."

"If that is true, then I hope he is with us."

"He is always on the side of the righteous, and this land belongs to Tillicoulty, not some king who lives several days' ride away and cares not for it."

Hamish strode along beside her, his breaths puffing out in front of him.

"Tyr represents defending what's yours even when it would be easier to surrender," Astrid went on. "He rises up and looks an opponent in the eye but does not back down because he knows his cause is the right one."

"Which is what we must do."

"*Ja*, that is what we must do." And it was the reason she was prepared to fight, possibly die. She wanted to be on the side of justice and freedom. Plus, there was no way she was going to let her brothers have sagas to tell afterward and she none.

The lur went quiet and Astrid saw Haakon on the watchtower looking down at the gathering villagers. He stood feet hip-width apart, surveying the newly trained warriors. Many of them had painted their faces with blue ink. Swirls and crosses and some had stripes over their eyes. They all held weapons and shields.

They came to a stop and Orm bounced up, his usual black kohl replaced with indigo around his eyes and down his nose, chin, and throat. He was excited for the fight—she could see it in his twitchy movements. "Here. Here." He daubed his finger in a pot of paint. "You must wear this." Quick as a flash, he drew a stripe over her nose, one cheek to the other.

"Get off." She frowned at him.

"No," Hamish said. "Let him do it. It will remind every villager that you are on the side of Tillicoulty." He dipped his finger into Orm's pot and coated the tip. He then filled one of his cheeks with color, so much that some of it dripped down the pale skin of his neck to the hollow of his throat.

"Is King Athol here?" Astrid asked Orm.

"No, not yet. But Knud took a ride out and saw his men prowling. They will arrive soon."

"Good." She nodded. "We can get into position."

"People of Tillicoulty," Haakon suddenly bellowed. "The time has come to defend our land and I, as your king, will serve you well, as will the men and woman who journeyed the northern seas to get here. We are at your service. We will be triumphant, and we will survive to see the sunset and a new day, a day of freedom from the man who has stolen from you." He banged his hand on his chest. "I know that in my heart. God is with you. The gods are also with us. We can and will win this battle. Know that with every tendon and sinew and bone and vein that holds your body together."

A cheer went up.

"And," he said, "we are prepared. We are using our brains as well as our bodies. Odin walks amongst us as a peasant soldier. He will guide us and give us strength." His voice rose. "And know this: just as Odin might be underestimated as a working man with a simple demeanor, King Athol will surely underestimate us. I, your king, have battled many times and each time, I have been victorious. That is not about to change." He withdrew his sword and banged it against his shield. "I can already taste my victory drink, I can already smell the blood of my enemy, and I can already hear their death screams."

The crowd cheered again.

"So," he said, pointing with his sword at the forest, "now is the time for us to carry out our plan. Everyone knows what to do, every man and woman has a task, an important task that when combined as one will see King Athol knocked from his false power." He stamped his foot. "Open the gates. We will greet our visitor out of the fort walls." He pointed at Noah. "My wise friend, you will take my place on the watchtower and defend the ramparts."

Noah nodded and started to walk with his cane, toward the tower.

The gates were thrown open and the villagers all but charged through them. Once on the other side, they dashed over the hard, mud-churned earth to take up position.

"Brother," Kenna said, appearing at Hamish's side. "I wish you Godspeed in battle."

He wrapped her in his arms, her blue-painted face pressing against his hard armor. "And you, beloved sister. I never thought we would face this day, but here we are."

She pulled back and touched his cheek. "Here we are." She swallowed, a small, gulping sound.

"You are a fine fighter, Queen Kenna," Astrid said. "Know that as you face each sword and let your instinct do the rest."

"I will try."

"He is here! He is here! King Athol has arrived," Orm shouted loudly as he hopped on the spot clapping.

"Come, we must go." Hamish gestured forward.

Kenna ran off with Orm toward Haakon. Astrid and Hamish rushed to take up their place beside the foliage-and-branch-covered ditch. They were to be part of the shield wall right in front of it, luring any surviving enemy to their death.

Haakon was now on Fen, a huge, black horse with thick feathers and a long, glossy mane. He kicked the creature on and it shook its head and broke into a trot, giving a whinny, as though also excited.

"There he is," Hamish said, nodding at the misty forest track to the west. "King Athol."

Astrid turned to see the king riding from the forest with a posse of men on foot behind him. They snaked from the trees, tracking the hoof prints of his stocky bay. At the rear was another horse, a gray, that appeared to be carrying a woman.

"He is wearing a crown," Astrid said. "That is a bold move."

"He is a bold man."

Their feet stamped on the mud. Astrid wondered if it would have been better if they'd had a frost. The earth was slippery and would make fighting even harder.

Haakon stopped just short of the hidden spiked fence, which lay flat and, like the ditch, was concealed with branches and muddy fir branches.

King Athol stopped too, about forty paces from Haakon. His men, about fifty in total, came to a standstill behind him. The gray horse came to a halt on his left flank.

The mist swirled, a raven cawed in the distance, and a village dog let out a long, desolate howl.

"You are on my land," Haakon shouted loudly. "What is your business here?"

"This is *my* land," King Athol called back, his voice sharp and accented. "And I have come to claim taxes from my people of Tillicoulty. They owe me."

"They are not your people and as I said, this is my land," Haakon called. "These people owe you nothing, nor do I."

King Athol raised his chin and stared at Haakon.

Fen shifted from one foot to another and flicked his tail. Haakon kept his attention firmly on King Athol.

"Who are you?" King Athol asked eventually.

"I am Haakon Rhalson, King of Tillicoulty."

"Ha, you are a delusional Norseman. You are not king. You are not anything. Go. Go and get in your boat and get the hell off my land."

Orm banged his sword against his shield. "Make us, old man."

King Athol swung his attention to Orm and then seemed to take in the rest of the villagers and the handful of Vikings. "Do you really think farmers will defeat my soldiers?"

"When men are fighting for something they are prepared to die for, you should never underestimate them," Haakon replied.

"Death"—King Athol touched his crown—"is exactly what will happen today. I will baste this land in your blood."

"Do not be so sure." Haakon glanced at Orm and then Gunner, who were in prime position to pull up the lethal sharp fence when the moment came.

"I am sure. I am sure that God is on my side. He sees me as the rightful king of these lands. He knows that I deserve to be paid for my generosity of spirit in letting these people farm and hunt and fish here."

"It is nature that provides, not you."

King Athol sneered. "I will give you one more chance to walk away or bow down to me. Which will it be?"

Haakon shook his head. "Neither."

Astrid felt a surge of pride. Her brother was completely undaunted by this Lothlend king, who looked as though he'd sucked on a bitter root.

"Dismount and get on your knee!" King Athol shouted. "I demand it, heathen."

"I am not a heathen. I am a Christian, like you." Haakon banged his chest with his fist.

"What? Why you... Of all the..." King Athol held up his sword. "Charge!"

A sudden roar filled the air along with the metallic slide of metal as swords were drawn. The surge of energy from Athol's men had anticipation racing through Astrid. They split in half, a section of them running at Haakon, not knowing that vicious, wooden spikes would soon be in their path, and the others ran at Astrid, Hamish, and the other villagers, soon to fall into a ditch, if the arrows and spears didn't get them.

It was time.

She tightened her grip on her sword and again checked her seax was in place.

"My God be with us," Hamish said.

"Fight well, my love."

"'My love'?" Hamish turned to her.

She scowled at him. It wasn't what she'd meant to say. "Just bloody fight and don't die." She raised her shield. "Shield wall!"

The group reacted instantly, dropping into position as archers fired a rain of arrows on the approaching enemy.

Several hit their target, men dropping to the mud with shouts of pain.

"Spears!" she shouted, glancing left and right at the frightened but determined faces in the shadows of their shields.

Again, several spears hit their targets.

The noise of the battlefield had picked up—screams, wails, and shouts. She guessed the spiked fence had been raised and hoped it had taken out many of their foes.

"Hold it. Hold it," Hamish shouted. "Keep the wall. Keep the wall." His knuckles were pale, as he was holding the handle of his sword so tight.

She swallowed, her mouth dry.

"Just a bit more…" Hamish said, almost to himself. "Another few…"

And they did have to keep their nerve. The warriors in the wall could see King Athol's men racing toward them with pikes and spears and swords.

"Nearly…" Hamish said through gritted teeth.

A sudden yelp of shock and pain signified the first of the enemy falling through the undergrowth and into the ditch.

Within seconds, there was another and another. Astrid peered between her shield and Hamish's and saw them dropping into the ditch as though falling into the jaws of Fenrir.

"Now!" Hamish yelled, dropping his shield from its protective position. "Kill them. Now!" He rushed forward with a roar, sword slashing. Fearless. Strong. Intimidating.

Astrid followed him into the battle. Her right foot slipped on the mud, but she quickly righted herself and took on a man trying to climb from the ditch. It took her only one swipe to finish him off.

The first of many.

Chapter Eighteen

THE BATTLE RAGED on with a clash of swords, spine-chilling yells, and the grunting cries of war.

Astrid spotted Kenna fighting hard and using her nimble body to outwit a tall and heavy soldier who was unstable on the mud. The queen took him down then rushed to the next with her bloodied sword at the ready.

Quickly, Astrid ducked as an arrow flew up from the ditch, narrowly missing her ear. She jabbed her sword into the dank quagmire and felt the satisfaction of a death blow as her blade hit flesh.

Pulling back, she slipped over, her hands and knees landing in the wet mud. But she jumped up, back straight, weapons at the ready. The ditch had done its magic, as had the spiked fence—the vast majority of Athol's men were down.

And Haakon was in hand-to-hand combat with King Athol himself.

She didn't fancy Athol's chances. Haakon was twice his size and in full kill mode. He swiped his sword through the air as though it were no heavier than a needle and his features were set in grim determination.

"Kill them all!" Orm shrieked to her right as he punched the air. "Kill them. *Drepe dem alle!* We will drink from their skulls to celebrate our victory."

A smash of metal on metal and a heavy grunt had her spinning around again—Hamish was being attacked by a huge Lothlend warrior with a cape of fur and mud and blood streaking over his face.

Hamish swung his sword upward to protect himself. Sparks flew. He then spun to the left, almost stumbling on the slippery surface, and aimed at his attacker's torso.

But for a big man, Hamish's opponent was fast and dodged out of the way. The next slice of his sword came fast and hard and glanced off Hamish's upper arm.

He yelled in anger through gritted teeth as blood poured from the wound. He went in for another strike, but this time, the mud took his feet and he half-fell into the ditch.

With her heart almost thudding out of her chest, Astrid charged forward to assist Hamish. With each step, her fear increased and her panic mounted. The monster had his sword raised again, ready to bring it down on Hamish's head, a lethal blow.

She summoned all of her strength, prayed that the gods were with her, and lunged forward, piercing the leather armor of the attacker right in the center of his back. He froze, arms aloft, sword angled at Hamish, and then, almost as if in a slow dream, he fell forward.

"Hamish!" she yelled, withdrawing her sword from the big man's back.

Hamish, with wide eyes, dashed to the right to avoid the heavy body dropping toward him.

"Are you all right?"

"Aye." He was breathing hard.

"Get out of there."

He hauled himself out of the body-filled ditch, blood from his wound mixing with the mud.

She grabbed his good arm and pulled him up. It wasn't easy with the thick mud gripping his boots.

"Blessed be to God," Hamish gasped, getting to his feet at her side. "Did you see the size of him?" He wiped a muddy hand over his cheek, leaving streaks of red and brown in the blue paint.

"He was a Lothlend berserker, I am certain."

"A what?"

"A soldier high on amanita or something similar." She was puffing for breath. "I saw one nearly take out Haakon once. 'Haps he is traveled from the North, like us, and took up with Athol for a fee."

She looked around, hands on her thighs. The men and women of Tillicoulty were indeed winning their battle.

"Kenna," Hamish gasped, suddenly rushing to the right. "Come."

Astrid followed. She could see what Hamish had seen. Three big men had rounded on Kenna and were showing no mercy.

Haakon saw it at the same time and with one devastating slice of his sword, he finished his battle with King Athol by taking his head from his neck. He then turned and roared and raced to his wife.

They all arrived at once and within seconds had taken out the three soldiers, leaving them dead and bleeding on the earth.

A spear was flying toward Astrid, barely moving, just getting bigger, the steely tip flashing through the milky mist. A woman had thrown it with deadly aim and stood still watching her weapon's journey.

"Fuck!" Astrid ducked and shifted to the left, barely avoiding it.

But the spear struck something—the clanging thud of metal on metal and then a splash.

She spun around. "Hamish!"

He'd landed in a puddle thick with mud and blood, his arms and legs akimbo and his eyes closed.

"No!" She dropped to his side and cupped his filthy face. "Hamish. Hamish. Wake up." Her heart squeezed as terror gripped her. "Please. No." She spun to Haakon. "She has killed him." She pointed at the woman. "That woman has killed my Hamish."

Haakon frowned then looked back at the treeline. "The woman. Get her. Quick."

"I will." Orm sprang into action. Like a dog chasing a hare, he pelted over the battlefield.

"Bitch!" Astrid said, searching Hamish for wounds. His upper arm was bleeding heavily. His helmet was still on, though there was a huge dent over the forehead.

Kenna rushed to Hamish's side. "The spear hit him there, but the helmet took the worst of the impact." She touched her own brow then dropped to her knees and clasped her brother's hand. "I saw it." She choked in a sob. "Hamish. Hamish. Wake up. Please don't be dead."

"We are victorious." Haakon grasped the king's head by the hair and held it aloft. "WE ARE VICTORIOUS!"

There was a scamper as the last few of Athol's men still alive ran for cover.

"Aye! We did it!" someone else yelled.

"Be off with you!"

"We won. Long live King Haakon!"

But Astrid couldn't celebrate. Her heart was tearing in two. Hamish had promised they would lie down together that night with blood and breath in their bodies. She glanced upward, looking for Valkyrie. Nothing, just the eerie blanket of fog that seemed to add to her confusion and pain and the dreams for her future slipping away.

"He is alive, but we need to get him inside," Kenna said with her fingertips on Hamish's neck.

"He is alive?"

"Aye."

Astrid stuttered out a breath. A tear broke free and tracked down her cheek. She never cried. It took her a moment to realize what the feeling was.

"Astrid." Kenna took her hand, mud squelching between their fingers. "He'll live. He's strong. Very strong. And he has something...*someone* to live for."

Kenna nodded and dashed at the tear, embarrassed by it, embarrassed about looking weak in front of her sister-by-marriage.

"The men will carry him." Kenna looked up. "Gunner, Ivar, Knud, where are you...?"

Gunner appeared, his face bloody and his sword stained ruby red. "He is alive?" He nodded at Hamish.

"Aye." Kenna tried to move Hamish. "But we need to get him inside. Where is—?"

"Egil is dead!" Knud ran up, half-slipping as he drew to a halt. He had a large cut in his leather armor. Someone had gotten close with their sword. "Egil is dead." He pointed to the right.

"Oh, no." Kenna clasped her hand to her chest. "Poor Egil."

Astrid swallowed the bitter taste of loss. "Do not be sad, Kenna. Egil will be flying upward with his Valkyrie as a champion. Tonight, he will sup with the gods and lie with virgins. He will not lament his death, for it is an honor to die in battle, so you must not lament it, either."

Kenna frowned. "I hope that is true." She looked up at Gunner. "Help me with Hamish. We do not want to lose more men."

Suddenly, Hamish was being hauled into the air by Gunner and Knud. His limbs dangled and his head lolled while his sword and shield fell to the ground.

"The king's head will go on a spike at the entrance to the fort along with the other fallen soldiers who tried to unjustly rule us," Haakon yelled. "Take the heads, good men and women of Tillicoulty. They are our spoils of war, along with our freedom!" He raised the severed head again and roared.

"And let that be a warning to others." Astrid glared at Athol's wide eyes, staring unseeing from his skull. "Bloody Christian idiot."

"I have her! I have her!" Orm strode from a thick patch of mist and into the group of panting, blood-stained, jubilant villagers who had surrounded Haakon. "The one who tried to get away. I have her."

He had a woman clasped by her wrists and was dragging her along. Her long, dark hair was caked in mud, as was her gown. She was hissing angry words at Orm and struggling to be free.

"Who is this?" Haakon said.

"A shield-maiden," Orm replied. "But not a very good one." He laughed manically.

"I will kill her," Astrid said, holding out her sword and marching up to the woman. "She threw the spear that hit Hamish."

"No, no, don't kill her," Orm said. "I need a thrall." He blocked Astrid's path. "I wish for a slave to wash my feet and cook my food."

"So find another one. This one needs to die."

"No." Haakon grabbed Astrid's arm. "Wait."

The woman suddenly screamed, her attention on the head in Haakon's right hand. "You monster. You monsters. What have you done to my father? What have you done to the king of all these lands? You will pay for this. You are the devil's work."

"Father?" Haakon said, holding the head closer to her. "This is your father?"

She screwed up her eyes and turned away. "Oh...Father... No... Please, no."

Astrid's blood boiled and her hand itched for the kill. She pulled in a deep breath and looked to the right, willing her self-control to come back. This prisoner might be worth more alive, she understood that. Princesses were currency.

A raven hopped in her peripheral vision, jumping over a body and then another before pecking at a corpse's slashed arm. "Odin," she whispered. "You are here. Watching us."

And then she saw him: a dark, stooped figure with a flowing hooded cape looming from the cold, wet air. It was Odin. Who else could it have been? He'd come to witness the bloodshed, the victory, the brave warriors who'd fought in his name. He'd come himself. His ravens had reported the battle and he'd come. Right now, the benches would be readied for a great banquet to rejoice in the spoils of war and he would listen to the tales, nodding, for he knew their truth—he'd seen it for himself.

She clutched the runestone purse on her belt as if trying to harness some of his presence within them. It was a privilege to witness a god, and not just any god, but Odin himself.

"Astrid. Astrid."

"What?" She turned to Haakon with a frown and then turned back to the mist.

Odin was gone.

"What?" she said again, irritated that she hadn't seen the All Father for longer but still in awe that she had at all.

"We'll keep her alive," Haakon said, "in case we need a bargaining tool. Do not kill her."

"*Ja, ja*, if that is what you want." She glanced at Hamish, who was being carried away at speed. "I have to...go..."

"Well, that's settled, then," Orm said, suddenly throwing the slight woman over his shoulder and clamping his right hand on her rear with a resounding slap. "I have a Lothlend slave." He laughed. "Just what I always wanted."

The woman squealed and kicked. "Get off me! I am a princess. I am not your slave." She beat her hands on Orm's back, but he just laughed harder and strode to the fort.

Astrid took off across the macabre pasture. The spikes and ditch had done their work, but it was a nasty mess to be cleared. And Egil, they would have to build a pyre and send him out to sea. But that would have to wait. Right now, she had a man to care for.

Her man.

"Take him to my dwelling," she ordered Gunner and Knud. "This way." She ran ahead, bidding them to follow with haste.

When they ducked inside, Hamish was still in a heavy sleep.

"On there. Lay him on there." She pointed at the wide straw cot they used for a bed.

While they did that, she added two more logs to the fire and set water over it.

"How bad is it?" Kenna ducked in.

"His arm is bleeding, but I do not think it is to the bone. And his head..." Gently, Astrid removed the helmet. "It appears unharmed, but...well...he's not here, is he?"

"Oh, dear Lord, have mercy." Kenna kissed the cross at her neck and sent her eyes upward.

"I will care for him," Astrid said. "Go and check on the rest of your family."

"But—"

"I am happy to."

"Are you sure?" Kenna frowned.

"*Ja*, of course I am sure, he is...mine too."

Kenna smiled, just a little. "I do believe he is, Astrid." She squeezed Astrid's shoulder. "Thank you. I will return, as will our mother."

She slipped out and Astrid set about removing Hamish's mud and blood-soaked armor. He lay heavy and unyielding and it was a difficult task. But eventually, she had his torso bare and his muddy boots off.

The gash on his arm was deep and she washed it thoroughly with warm water to better see the extent of the damage and get rid of the mud.

Stitches and poultice were needed.

Quickly, she sought out supplies, threaded a needle with animal sinew and pinched the wound edges together. She began to create a series of knots, washing the blood away that was still leaking from it. Every now and then, she glanced up at his face, but he was still sleeping.

"Please, Freya, let him wake up. Do not let him be in a death sleep." She blinked rapidly, refusing to let herself cry again, and carried on stitching.

"What? What are you doing?"

Fion, Hamish's mother, appeared. Her face was pale and her eyes wide. "In the name of God..."

"I am fixing him." Astrid continued her meticulously neat stitches. "Have you not seen this before?"

"Sewing a man's flesh…" She shook her head. "No."

"It is done many times after battle." Astrid nodded at a shelf. "Can you get some honey? I will coat it before I bandage it."

Fion rushed to get the honey and set it beside the bandage Astrid had laid out. "Oh, Hamish. What happened? Why is he…asleep?"

"A spear hit his helmet." Astrid frowned. "We must ask the gods to wake him up. Perhaps he is dreaming of Valhalla and all the delights he will receive there."

"I would imagine he's dreaming of heaven," Fion said, straightening Hamish's cross, which had been lying at an angle near his throat.

Astrid said nothing.

"Oh, merciful Lord, please do not take my son." Fion clasped her hands together beneath her chin.

"He'll wake up," Astrid said, finishing the last stitch.

"Oh…but… Oh, please, pray with me. God must surely hear us."

"I won't pray with you." Astrid looked at Fion. "Because your god is not my god. But I will tell you he will wake up. His time on this earth is not done."

"I wish I had your certainty." Fion sobbed as tears fell down her cheeks. She clasped Hamish's hand.

"I am certain."

"But how…?" Her eyes were glassy with tears. "How do you know, Astrid?"

"Because he will give me sons." There. She'd said it.

Fion's mouth hung open. "What?"

"I have received a prophecy, from not just my mother, but the goddess Freya herself. I will bear three sons by Hamish McCallum of Tillicoulty who will become fine warriors and skilled seafarers. So…" She touched her belly. "Even if one is here already, there are another two he must make." Astrid set the needle aside and reached for the honey.

"I… You…and…?" Fion's eyes misted as she crossed her chest.

Astrid gave a huff of amusement at the strange Christian ways and began to slather honey onto the wound to fight away the green-and-yellow disease that festered in dirty battle wounds.

"I…" Fion's eyes were wide and her mouth like a fish's out of water. "But…he…is… And…"

"Your son is no longer a virgin, if that is what you are asking." Astrid glanced at his face thinking of how he looked when full of desire. She wanted him like that again. She'd do anything for it. "He is a man who lies with a woman with passion and fights battles with bravery. His sons will be kings, great kings. This is something you should understand. He is not your infant boy anymore. He is not a mild farmer of your gentle land. The gods have other plans for him, and this is just the first."

Chapter Nineteen

"MAY THE LORD have mercy on your heathen soul." Fion stared at Astrid.

"I do not need your lord's mercy." Astrid squeezed out a fresh strip of linen and began to wipe Hamish's face. It was awash with blue paint, drying mud, and crusting blood. "I have my own gods who look upon me favorably."

"You have corrupted my son. My only son." She clasped her hands in prayer.

Astrid felt her temper sparking to life. She turned to Fion. "I have shown your son what it is to be a man, what it is to live beyond the fortress walls of Tillicoulty. On this very day, I have saved his life, a fact that cannot be argued with. And now...now I care for him with all the devotion of the goddess Eir, who will this very moment be healing him through my hands." Her jaw tensed and her heart thudded as she rinsed out the cloth and turned back to Hamish.

"You must be married." Fion stood. "Now. I will fetch Olaf the priest."

"You will do no such thing."

"It is not your decision. I cannot have my son die after lying with you and him be an unwed soul."

Astrid carried on washing Hamish's face with tender strokes of the cloth. "You are wasting your breath. I am not the marrying kind."

"You will have to be, child."

Astrid's temper flared like a fast-rising wave in a storm. "Do not 'child' me. I am not your child. I am Princess Astrid Rhalson of Drangar." She pointed at Fion. "And nobody, *nobody*, least of all a meek, Lothlend, Christian woman tells me what to do or to get married."

"Well, of all the…" Fion crossed herself again. Her cheeks had reddened.

"You should leave before you are further shocked. I will care for your son in the Viking way because…as I have discovered, he likes how Vikings do things…especially how a Viking lady does things late at night, in the dark when clothes are gone and lust runs high."

Fion gasped and stumbled backward. Then she fled out the door.

Astrid laughed softly, glad to be alone with Hamish again. She rinsed out the cloth. The water was dirtying now, so she tossed it out and refilled it.

"That was wicked, you know."

"Hamish!" She bumped down on the side of the bed again and cupped his cheek. "You are awake?"

He cleared his throat and winced. "I have been awake for the last few minutes but decided to stay out of that particular conversation."

"How… How do you feel? Your head?"

Gingerly, he used his unharmed arm to touch his brow. "There is a lump."

"*Ja,* and a bruise. That's what happens when you get hit in the head with a spear."

He studied her with a frown.

"What? Are you seeing two of me?"

He laughed and then groaned. "No, thank goodness. The world can only cope with one of you."

She smiled and tipped forward, brushing her lips with his. "I think you will be well soon."

"Aye." He glanced at the door. "What happened?"

"Haakon killed King Athol. He took his head. Tillicoulty was victorious. There will be no more tribute-collecting by greedy kings who live far away."

"That is good."

"And the woman who threw the spear that hit you, it was Athol's daughter. Orm has taken her as a slave."

"A slave. The first in Tillicoulty." He raised his eyebrows.

"They are very useful, if you have one with some intelligence but little spirit." She shrugged. "But I suspect this one has spirit."

He was staring at her.

"What?" she asked.

"You're filthy, Astrid."

Glancing downward, she saw he was right. She'd cleaned him but not herself. "I will get you some bread and ale then wash."

"Aye, I think that would be good." He pushed himself to sitting, being careful with his arm.

"I stitched and bandaged that wound." She nodded at it and passed him food and drink.

"'Stitched'?"

"*Ja*, with a yarn needled and animal sinew. It will hold the cut together while it heals, then we can remove it." She set her armor aside and then removed her boots. Her feet were relatively clean as she stood on the woven rug beside the fire. "Did you enjoy the battle?"

"'Enjoy the battle'?"

"*Ja*, you trained for it, dressed for it. Did you enjoy it?" She removed her helmet, pants, and tunic.

"It was violent and brutal and I hope I never have to see so much bloodshed again."

"Oh, Christian boy." She laughed and shook her head. "What kind of sons will you make with that attitude?"

"Ones who value life but know when, why, and how to fight." He sipped his ale.

She paused and studied him. "Maybe that's not so bad."

"Kenna is well?"

"*Ja*, she fought like a true shield-maiden. You should be proud." She paused. "But Egil is dead, taken by the Valkyrie to feast in Valhalla this very eve."

Hamish paused, chewing his bread. "I am sorry." He touched his cross. "He was a good and brave man and joined our cause."

"It was his cause too. He lived here and my brother was his king."

"He will be buried?"

"No." She dropped the last of her clothes to one side and scooped warm water into her hands, stooping and washing her face over the bowl. "He will be set alight on a floating pyre and sent out to sea with treasures."

"'Set alight'?"

"*Ja*, he was a great seafarer and died a great warrior. It only fair that his mortal body is sent to the gods with a generous bounty."

"And where will you get this generous bounty?"

"I am sure Haakon will think of something." She washed her face again. It felt good—she'd been caked in mud. After she'd dried it, she looked at Hamish.

He was studying her intently, the way he always did when she was naked. "You'd better hope no one comes in here."

"They'll get a treat if they do." She wriggled her bare ass.

"You're wicked, you know that?" He laughed then moaned and touched his head.

"That bad?" She set to work cleaning the rest of her body.

"Not so bad that I don't still want you when I see you like that." He shifted on the bed.

She said nothing and let her eyeline run down his chest to his groin.

"My cock still works. No battle damage there, if that is what you were wondering."

"I wasn't, but…" She wiped the cloth over her breasts, her nipples hardening.

"But what?"

"It might be a nice way to celebrate surviving the battle. It would make a change from drinking ale from the skulls of the dead."

His eyes widened. "You... You really do that?"

She threw her head back, her hair coming free, and laughed. "*Ja*, but not fresh skulls. They need drying out. I will show you later."

"Please don't." He set his ale aside and tapped his lap. "Come here. Let me thank you properly for killing that big bastard who tried to take me out in the ditch."

"I *did* save your ass." She walked over to him, sashaying her hips with each step.

"You are a fine warrior. I was proud of you."

"You were?" She straddled him and set her hands on his shoulders.

"Aye. Proud that you're mine." He cupped her nape and pulled her in for a kiss. It was a possessive, dominant hold, but she liked it and sighed and closed her eyes. If it was Hamish who wanted to possess her, then she could live with that. But only him. No one else.

"I am so glad we're both alive," he murmured onto her lips. "I don't think I could breathe without you."

"And my heart would stop without you," she said, pushing his damp hair from his face.

He smiled. "That is enough."

"What do you mean?"

"I know you'll never be my wife, Astrid. But to know I'm in your heart—that is enough."

"You *are* my heart." Her eyes prickled again with those pesky tears and she kissed him harder and squeezed her eyes closed.

He moaned softly and slid his big hand down her back and up again.

But slow and sensuous wasn't what she wanted. She wanted him inside her. So she fumbled with his pants and freed his cock.

His erection was thick and solid and her pussy quivered as she took it in her fist and swiped her thumb over his slit.

"Ride me," he murmured. "You're so good at that."

"I know." She lifted up and positioned herself over him.

He glanced at the doorway as he gripped her waist.

"Hey." She turned him to face her again. "That's not your view. I am."

"But what if someone comes in?"

"Like I said, they'll get a treat and they'll know for sure that I am a great healer and you are well and truly alive."

His eyes sparkled and his mouth twitched into a grin. "There is no one like you in all of these lands."

"There is no one like me in *my* lands, either."

"Can these be your lands?"

"For now." She lowered onto him, taking him into her wet heat.

"I will go wherever you go," he said, his voice strained as she took him deeply.

"Then you will have a life full of adventure and many sons." Her ass hit his legs and she tipped her head back, relishing the dense invasion that hit all her sweet spots just right.

He kissed her neck, nibbling gently, and cupped her right breast with one hand.

"Oh, so good," she gasped, feeling everything in exquisite detail—her hair swishing on her bare back, her ass on the material of his pants, her nipples so tight and tingling. Every part of her body was so alive, on fire. The battle had heightened her senses and filled her with energy. Victory was the very sap of life.

"You feel so good," he murmured.

"So do you." She moved her hips, rubbing herself against him. "Oh...Hamish."

"Take what you need."

"I will. I am." She crushed against him then rocked away, her hips dancing as her nub was stimulated. She held his wide shoulders, her fingers digging into his muscles.

He sucked in a breath through gritted teeth and closed his eyes. His cock was as hard as it got. War had clearly given him the same power rush—a close brush with death making life all the more satisfying.

She worked him harder, grinding faster. The pressure was growing, the need to come would soon be upon her.

"Ah...don't stop..." he said, looking at her again. There was color in his cheeks now. "I'm so... Are you?"

"I'm close too. Let's come. Together." She slanted her head and kissed him as she hugged his cock with her pussy.

She caught his moan in her mouth and mixed it with her own. His arms were tight around her, his hips moving up to meet hers.

The pressure couldn't be contained and she didn't want it to be. With full control, she let herself hover on the brink of climax for a few honeyed beats and then spiraled into ecstasy.

He cried out, a gruff and unholy praise, and released into her. His cock throbbed around her spasming pussy and the hot wetness of his seed soaked into her.

Still she moved on him, taking every bit of pleasure. Her heart beat wildly, her pulse thudded in her ears. And he stayed with her, his kiss intense and urgent, as though he needed her more than he needed anything else in his life.

"Hamish," she gasped, their chests slicking together. "Oh...that was good..."

"I fear war has...given me...an appetite for you."

"You were already pretty hungry for it."

He laughed. "For you, aye. I'm always hungry for you."

She slowed and stopped, not ready to lift off him. "We should agree not to lie with anyone else."

He raised his eyebrows. The bump on his head was darkening

now. "Do you *want* to lie with someone else?"

"No." She paused. "But I don't want you to, either."

He smiled and pushed her hair from her face. "You are my one and only lover, Astrid, and if I die that way, I will be a happy man."

"Do you mean that?"

"Aye, you are everything I need and more. So much more."

She smiled. "Good, that is agreed, then."

"Agreed."

Chapter Twenty

E GIL'S BODY WAS set upon a large, wooden raft created by Gunner, Ivar, and Knud and attached to the small pier in Eliah Bay.

As they'd worked, Orm had played a skin-topped drum in a thick, deep rhythm that resembled a heartbeat. He'd painted the top half of his face black and had his new slave at his side. Her ankles were chained together so that when she walked it was a slow shuffle and she huddled within a huge, dark fur.

Astrid clutched her small purse holding the runestones and stared out at the horizon. Usually, such a grand burial was reserved for noblemen and kings, but she understood why Haakon had insisted upon it. Egil had been a nobleman in Tillicoulty. Without him, they'd never have even gotten to Lothlend. Every hand on deck had been necessary.

The day was darkening with heavy clouds and the chill in the air nipped her cheeks. Soon, there'd be more snow. It would be a relief from the rain and mud.

Was her father still alive? She closed her eyes and his face hovered before her—lined and old, his eyes full of wisdom and love. She sighed and drew her hood up.

"Are you well?" Hamish asked, slipping his good arm around her waist and pulling her closer. His other was held up in a sling.

"Ja, I was thinking of my father." She pointed to the horizon. "Wondering if he was still out there, over the water, breathing, eating, laughing with Ravn and his family."

"Can you feel him in your heart?"

"Always." She smiled. "He'll always be in my heart."

"He is a lucky man. It is not an easy place to get into." He pressed a kiss to her head, over her hood.

They stood quietly together. The beat of the drum seemed to vibrate through the ground, to the soles of her feet and up into her body. How strange it was that her family had become so fractured. The gods must have had too much ale when they'd mapped that path.

Haakon, Gunner, and Knud began to lay items around Egil's body. It had been set on wood, then furs that were decorated with glossy mistletoe sprigs.

"What are they doing with all that stuff?" Hamish asked.

"They are grave goods. Things he will find useful in his next life."

Among the items were Egil's sword and shield, his helmet and armor. There was a jug of ale and a tankard, his cape and iron brooch shaped like a longboat. A loaf of bread and several apples, his belt folded neatly and atop it his arm ring, which had been polished.

"That will all go out to sea?" Hamish asked.

"Out to sea and then to Valhalla. The flames will take it there as they rise upward."

Kenna lit several baskets of logs along the pier and they sprang to life, fanned by the wind.

The small crowd huddled closer.

The drum beat.

Haakon kissed Kenna's cheek and took the torch from her. He turned to the crowd.

"Good people of Tillicoulty, today we honor our dead. Those in the churchyard and those, like Egil son of Daneson of Drangar, who take a different route to their eternal life." He paused and surveyed the villagers.

They all looked on with wide eyes, some sporting bandages and all huddled into their capes. Eight lives had been lost in total, all men, all brave warriors.

"To die in battle is to die with honor," Haakon went on, striding down the pier. He held his torch aloft. "It is to die leaving a legacy on Earth that your memory will never fade. To die for a cause, a belief, is to die for a reason and there is no greater reason than freedom." He shouted the last word.

A cheer went up.

"And as my friend, Olaf, has, with his sword, committed Christian bodies to God, I now commit Egil to the gods who await him in Valhalla." He raised his head, flashing his thick chin and neck tattoo. "Feast well, my friend. Feast well."

"This is all wrong." A sudden anger swelled in Astrid and she pushed from Hamish and strode forward. Her feet stomped on the wooden pier as she marched up to Haakon. "Give me that."

Haakon frowned at her as she went on tiptoes and snatched the torch. "What are you doing?"

"I am lighting the pyre." She glared at him, her eyes narrowed. "You are a Christian, are you not, brother?"

"I am." His jaw tensed. "I am also your king. Do not forget that."

"How could I ever?" She strutted past him, making for the raft that held Egil's body.

"Astrid," Haakon called. "Stop."

She drew alongside the body bobbing on the water. "Stop? Why? So you can light the pyre?"

"I am king." He strode up to her.

"And I am a believer. You have forsaken Odin and Thor and Freya. You do not even believe Egil is going to Valhalla."

He glanced at Kenna and then Noah, who stood on the beach with Fion and Olaf. "How can you say that?" he asked quietly through clenched teeth.

"Because I saw you renounce your heathen sins in this very bay." She held the torch over the body.

"Odin was watching over us in battle," Haakon said with a scowl. "That is why we won."

"*Ja*, but did you see him?"

"What?"

"Did you see Odin?" she asked.

"No…I…"

"I did." She jabbed her chest. "I saw him. He came to me. His raven too. That is because he knows that I court his favor. I make sacrifices to him. I follow his path, the path of destiny that he and all the gods have laid out for me. You have gone off that path. You have refused it."

"I have not. The path led me to Kenna and Tillicoulty."

She made a scoffing sound that rasped her throat in the cold air.

"And that path has led you to Hamish," he said.

"Do not speak of Hamish to me."

"Why not?" He raised his eyebrows in the maddening way he always did when he thought he knew something about her she didn't want him to know.

She rested her hand on her belly. "Because it is none of your business."

His mouth opened and closed as his attention drifted down her body.

"I am going to send Egil on his way," she said.

"Are you with child?" Haakon asked.

"What?" She snatched her hand from her belly.

"Are you carrying Hamish's child?"

"I have no idea." She used the torch to gesture at Haakon. The leaping flames danced, leaving a trail of black smoke.

He took a pace back to avoid being burned.

"And it is nothing to do with you, brother. So do not speak of it."

"You are my sister. It has everything to do with me."

She gritted her teeth so hard, she feared they might break. She looked past Haakon at Hamish standing on the beach. The stiff wind pressed his cape to his tall, strong frame and licks of bright hair curled from his dark hood.

"I will not marry him and he knows that."

"He is a brave man."

"Why do you say that?"

"Oh, come on, Astrid." Haakon huffed. "In Drangar, you reduced every man who ever wanted you to a quivering wreck. If Hamish hasn't run off nursing his wounds from your sharp tongue, then he is indeed a man worthy of you."

"He is not scared of me." Astrid scowled and pursed her lips.

"Good." Haakon smiled and something in his eyes softened despite the reflection of the flames dancing there. "Now, sister, will you send Egil on his way? He was a good friend to us both and a fine warrior to have at our side."

"And a strong seafarer to journey with." She turned to the body on the raft. "Hail to the gods. Hail to the dead!" she shouted so that everyone could hear. "Hail to the kinsmen, the family, the shields and the swords. Long may Egil's memory live in the minds of the living and his bravery and wisdom be rejoiced as he sits in the mighty halls of Valhalla."

She tossed the torch onto the body.

Instantly, the mistletoe leapt into flame along with the sacking used as a pillow for Egil.

Gunner and Knud released the ropes and Ivar gave the raft a shove with his foot.

The current caught it immediately, the receding tide bobbing it this way and that.

Hamish was suddenly behind her, his arms winding around her waist as he pulled her back to his chest. He didn't speak, just held her as the body went up in flames. Great licks of red, yellow, and orange that pierced the steel-gray sky.

She pictured the great halls in a realm she knew she'd see eventually—the gods, the brave warriors and shield-maidens, the sumptuous feast prepared by Andhrímnir each day anew.

The raft was caught on a gust of wind. It stoked the flames, the sound of their roar catching on the rushing air and filling her ears. The whole thing was alight now. A beacon in the vast, gloomy sea.

Kenna stepped past her, her scarlet cape flapping in the wind. "Look!" She pointed east of the pyre raft. "Someone is coming our way."

Haakon spun around.

So did Astrid.

On the horizon was a longboat. Its sails were red and its bow curved in the shape of a snake or dragon's head; it was hard to tell from this distance.

"Norsemen," Hamish snapped. "More of your sort."

"What is making them come here? Why not to the richer lands?" Haakon said.

"'Haps they want your crown," Hamish said.

Haakon swung a look at Hamish. "I will defend my crown as I defend this village."

"I do not dispute that," Hamish said, "only that another battle is something we should prepare for."

"You are right." Haakon drew his sword. "Get ready, men." He turned to the crowd. "Warriors, arm yourself. We have company."

While the hustle of villagers sounded behind her, Astrid withdrew her sword, wishing she also had her shield with her.

As the burning raft went farther into the distance, the longboat drew closer.

Soon, she saw that the front of the boat was a serpent with a long, forked tongue that seemed to lick the wind. She frowned. Did she recognize it?

"In the name of all the gods..." Haakon turned to look at her. "Can you see?"

Orm beat the drums to a crescendo, the sound booming around the bay. He then threw the sticks aside and raced down the pier, his footsteps clattering. "Thor's thunder rumbles around a crown!" he shouted. "It rumbles and it strikes with lightning…and here is the lightning." He came to a halt at her side, breathing hard. "Here is the lightning come to light us up."

"I… What the…?" Astrid untangled from Hamish and stepped forward, past Haakon, to the end of the pier.

Standing on the front of the boat with his arm wrapped around the neck of the serpent, white wolf fur flapping, was a man she knew only too well.

A man she'd never thought she'd see again.

A king she detested.

A brother she despised.

Her throat dried and her heart thudded. Confusion spun in her mind. "What the fuck is Ravn doing here?"

"I have no idea." Haakon puffed up his chest and tapped the tip of his sword onto the pier. "But there better be a bloody good reason."

"*Ja*, I know the reason. It is the gods' great plan for the skein of my life." Astrid tightened her grip on the handle of her sword. "He is here so I can kill him."

About the Author

Based in the UK, Lily Harlem is an award-winning, *USA Today* bestselling author of sexy romance. She's a complete floozy when it comes to genres and pairings, writing saucy historical, heterosexual kink, gay paranormal, and everything in between. She's also very partial to a happily ever after.

If you're a Kindle Unlimited subscriber, you can read many of her books for free, including several complete series, and if you love sporty romances, get the first novel in her popular HOT ICE series when you sign up for her newsletter.

One thing you can be sure of, whatever book you pick up by Ms. Harlem, is it will be wildly romantic and deliciously sexy. Enjoy!

Website: www.lilyharlem.com
Amazon Author Page: author.to/LilyHarlem
Lily's Reader Group: facebook.com/groups/188731774881774

Find your next book boyfriend…
Male/Female
Male/Male
Historical Romance
Paranormal
Menage a Trois
Reverse Harem
Audio Books

For more deliciously steamy historical romance, including a plethora of stern Highlanders, dashing dukes, and kinky Vikings, visit Lily's website.

Made in the USA
Las Vegas, NV
10 July 2025